My first novel,

for Izaak and Helen

PART ONE

There are mornings when a sudden shaft of silvery light striking a night-soaked mountain arouses an inexplicable, ineffable surge of delight and we remember, all too briefly, the abiding truth of the turning world. On such a morning the spirits of a man sitting hunched up against the early autumn chill on the slopes of Ben Dhu are uplifted as he watches and waits for a sighting of the golden eagle he hopes will come.

John Stewart is well protected from the mountain air. He has positioned himself on a wide ledge with his back pushed into the curve of the hillside and with his eyes facing eastwards. Behind him and out of sight at the back of the Ben, a loch fingers out westwards towards the open sea, but his situation shelters him from the westerly gathering moisture as it brushes across the surface of the water in the loch and sprays the slopes of a horseshoe range of hills which undulate around the Ben.

The man settles. He is patient. He knows how to be still, how to merge into the landscape so that any raptor casting a glance towards him will not be alarmed. His breathing slows to a comfortable rhythm and his mind sinks into a half-sleeping, semi-conscious state not exactly of thinking, for thought implies a degree of mental deliberation, more meditation in which recent experiences, remembered feeling mostly uncomfortable and unsatisfactory conclusions flicker in and out. His thoughts recall his recent appointment as Director of the newly created

Centre of Highland Wildlife and the lies he has told about his marital status. Perhaps they weren't really lies for wasn't it possible that Kate would bring the girls and they would make a fresh start? The trustees had welcomed the thought of two more children in the local school.

In his heart, however, John believes that this will not happen. Kate has gone too far this time. He has kept her intermittent affairs to himself, not even confiding in his sister Mary, (especially just now) who isn't quite sure what is happening, just grateful that he stays with her and her boys Alistair and David until his accommodation at the Centre is finished. Her husband Donald's death last January has come hard for all of them. The swiftness of his end had caused a shock wave through the village for he had seemed a strong man, a steady dependable worker in the Forestry Commission and well liked by everyone. Mary looks hollow now and the boys are querulous, unhappy. Best to keep his own pain private, provide support, and be the cheerful uncle promising fishing trips as soon as his new duties allow. But he is missing his girls back in Edinburgh with Kate.

Such are the half thoughts which swirl in John's mind as he sits on that cold ledge on Ben Dhu and so it is that when the first streaks of silver and lemon scour marks in the darkness he is surprised by the moment and as dawn sharpens his spirits become uplifted and upheld.

He shifts his position a little. It will be a short autumn, he thinks. The birches are already stripped of their leaves and the past few mornings have brought a lacing of white frost on the high tops of the range. He scans the sky for the wide confident sweep of a raptor emerging from the shadows, taking control again of its territory and seeking the first meal of the day. John hasn't eaten yet either but just then the whole of the eastern sky opens up before him and colours of rose, apricot, gold and peach pearl into one another in a glorious painted sfumato that casts a warm glow over the hill-tops. Hunger is forgotten; suddenly there is a sense of the possibility of all things good.

The eagle does not come and eventually John stretches and stamps his feet and carefully begins the descent. Mary will be up by now, reviving the fire and switching on the lamps. Soon the boys will be leaving their warm beds, reluctantly at first as sleep tugs at them to return to their intermittent dreams, but then coming down for their porridge, bickering and troubled.

The sky is lightening now in the east but yet still inky blue over the village and the sea. The man decides to use a different route, as he wants to view the loch from above, to enjoy the first glints of silver above the rim of the Ben as they flicker over the water. He watches his steps in the shadows here, and the contrasts of light and shade and the growing brightness behind him confuses his eyes, so it is a while before he notices a movement at the loch's edge below him, but even from here, is this a trickery of light? He can see a fiery shock of hair and with a start realizes he is seeing a woman, quite naked and quite alone, facing the dark waters. He is above and behind her and using his binoculars he watches as she moves nearer the water and slowly wades in, her slight and ghostly pale figure diminishing as it

7

disappears. In a rush of thoughts John remembers his sister telling him about the old croft's sale and restoration; that a woman is living there alone, that nobody knows much about her except that Jennie McCleod, the postie, had spoken to her... said she was a craftswoman of some kind, a tailor, or spinner or weaver; that she rarely comes into the village, her supplies are delivered...all this and a lurching heart as he continues to watch, helpless as she flounders silently below him, knowing that he will not be able to reach her in time.

But he must try. An instinct makes him move, travelling as speedily as possible and having to take his sight away from her to where his feet are already finding their own way down. The descent is made and John runs against the force of the wind to come at last to the side of the Lochhead Croft House and to the edge of the water. She is gone! The water chops as the breezes rake across and there is absolutely no sign of the woman at all. Urgently he examines the loch with his binoculars but there is nothing, only the slate grey waters rising and swelling and falling and he has not reached her in time.

A dull, cold feeling spreads from his stomach. He stands, forlorn. What terrible event has befallen him, entering his life like a thunderbolt, and the remembrance of his wife's infidelities and rejection of him floods his mind, this, too, another rejection; another reminder that he is a failure as a man.

But what is this? A light from a lamp inside the croft house flickers on, and passing in front of the unshuttered window, the figure of a woman wearing a dressing gown and with that unmistakable splash of red hair glides through the room.

John is rooted in the shadows outside. His breathing is hard and rasping. He cannot move. His feeling of desolation swiftly turns to anger. What on earth does she think she is playing at? He stares at the lighted window, his rage spilling out. What business has she in frightening him so? What is she thinking of, taking off her clothes and wading into the freezing waters at this time of day, at this time of year? Doesn't she know the cold could stop her heart, that she might drown and all the trouble that might bring...ambulances, police, statements, autopsies, court visits...the notoriety for the village, himself as the new Director...

And then, as he stares with anger towards the croft house, it occurs to him that were she to look out and see him there it could be her turn to be afraid. It might seem to her that his motives were suspicious. He takes some deep breaths. This is none of his business. He has enough troubles. He turns sharply and heads south towards the road.

***

"Here you are John! Sit yourself down and eat some porridge. It's just ready." Mary bustles around him, glad to be up and doing for she has dreamed badly in the night and is heartened to see her brother return.

"Where have you been Uncle John?" demands David. John affectionately scuffs the top of the young boy's curly hair. David is fair like his mother, whilst Alistair, with his darker hair and colouring and even features favours the father. Both boys listen as he tells them of his dawn vigil on the Ben. Like most youngsters hereabout a deep knowledge of their surroundings is absorbed almost unconsciously from infancy but it is knowledge taken for granted and so seems unimportant. He, as new Director of the Centre for Highland Life had a responsibility first and foremost he had said at his interview, to protect and nourish that knowledge and the local folk come first in his priorities; tourists second. This had gone down well with the panel but John had meant it, for it was the people who lived and worked the land and sea here who mattered most. Without them nothing was nurtured or remembered and their goodwill was paramount.

The boys are soon away to the sitting room, pushing and provoking each other as they gather their things for school. Mary sighs. They are becoming a handful she knows and is angry for a moment that Donald has died, leaving her to cope. He would have known how to calm them with a joke or just the right words.

"Mary, who is that woman living at Lochhead croft? I saw her from the Ben."

He is about to tell her of the incident but decides against it.

"Where's she from and what is she doing here? What is a lone woman doing, out there two miles from the village? Where's her man?"
John needs to satisfy his curiosity.

"Well, I did tell you a while back but I guess you were not listening."

Mary wonders if anyone listens to her these days. "Her name is Alice Brooks. Jennie told me. She's the only one who seems to know much about her. She comes from Edinburgh I think, on her own, no family apparently, and has set herself up as a weaver, not for passing trade, she gets orders and commissions and keeps herself to herself. Her materials come by road and the shop delivers her food supplies. I've packed boxes myself and every now and then she goes off to Edinburgh, I'm told to see people about her work. It's all very arty-tapestries and hangings for private collectors and corporate organizations. She's no making scarves and throws."

John takes more toast. He is still angry. He might have injured himself coming down the mountain as fast as that, just when he is starting a new job. That wouldn't look well at all. He is rattled. Women, he could do without them he thinks. Abruptly he gets up and reaches for his jacket. "I'm away until supper. The board rep is coming in. What are your hours today?"

Mary is quiet. "I'm in the shop until lunchtime and after that I'm to go to see the Minister about the memorial for Donald." John is ashamed that he has forgotten that it is today that the bench in Donald's memory is being planned.

"I'm sorry Mary. I forgot. Shall you be OK? Shall I come with you? I can cancel the board rep."

"I'll be fine John, no need for you to alter your plans." She is moving breadcrumbs across the tablecloth with the palm of her hand. "Its just Alistair. David wants to come on after school and help with the lettering but Alistair refuses, says it's a stupid idea,his Dad never sat on a bench anyway."

"It's still not long after, Mary. Alistair misses his

dad terribly.He's thirteen, it's an awkward age especially for a boy. He'll come round, give him time." And Mary clears away the breakfast things with a clattering. John shouts to the boys that he is away hand feels a little relieved that it is so.

***

Weeks pass and John is busy with the organization of the Centre. He has been right, autumn was short, a blaze of gold and russet as rowan, birch and hazel flared and shed their leaves and suddenly it is quite dark by 4.00pm. At night the temperatures dip sharply and mornings bring the fine glitter of frost. The streets of the village are empty in the evenings, only leaves and tree debris skittering in the wind. Once or twice he ventures to the pub and stands at the bar with his pint. A few of the village men drift in and out and old Dorrie Flint nurses her drink in the corner next to the fire. He leans against the bar reprising in his head the work of the day. Malcolm, the publican, grits and snorts as he leers at a tabloid image. His bull neck pushes his head forwards in an aggressive posture. He has a thick, bruised looking mouth.

"I'll bet she's a good lay." His lips are wet. "What do you say John?" John glances at the full page 'pin-up' the usual nearly naked girl with overblown breasts, pouting lips and a direct stare. Her face is dwarfed by an enormous head of red, curly hair and John finds himself thinking of the woman by the loch whose white limbs had seemed a little too thin and frail, creating a ghostly silhouette against the blackness of the water. Malcolm's lewd question disturbs him. A good lay is really what he could do with himself just now!

"Aye," he says. "She'll do." But really he is not at all attracted to the girl in the photograph. Sex with her would not be real somehow. Afterwards, she would disappear. He is wondering instead what it would feel like to hold the other woman, pale and shivering in his arms and is unsettled by the way his body is influencing his thoughts.

"Who's the woman at Lochhead croft?" he asks Malcolm. "I thought I saw her from the Ben a few weeks ago, but I've not seen her in the village." His curiosity defeats the voice of experience, which tells him to protect his thoughts from the likes of Malcolm McKenzie. There is a moment's pause within which the expression on Malcolm's face changes from satisfaction to sourness.

"Brooks. Her name is something Brooks. Margaret had it from Jennie McCleod. Ann or Lisa or something." His face glowers. "She's a stuck-up outsider from Edinburgh, never comes near us. She's no business to be buying and changing our property," he speaks as if Lochhead croft is his own. "And what is she doing out there all alone? No fucking use to the village. There's something fishy about it if you ask me, but our Margaret will find out."

John is struck by the malice in Malcolm's voice. Is he too regarded as an outsider? He also comes from Edinburgh and only his sister's marriage to a local gives him some acceptance here. And yet the new Centre will bring business to the village, especially the pub.

There is silence now. Only old Dorrie sucks at her clay pipe and Malcolm stacks glasses from a tray. A telephone rings and Margaret calls "The brewery again for you," and catching Malcolm's mood as she comes into the bar she picks up a polishing cloth and lowers her head.

"How's Mary doing, John?" her question is kind but her voice is hard.

"She's managing fair, thank you Margaret." He is polite but actually lies. You don't tell Margaret McKenzie anything to give cause for gossip. He'll protect his sister from village tongues if he can. Her depression worries him but only the likes of the Minister and his wife will know how she's struggling and be able to support her. What can the McKenzies and their two louts of sons do for her?

Feeling thoroughly out of sorts now, John drinks up the remaining mouthful of beer and bids anyone within earshot a goodnight. He'll go back to Mary's, make sure Alistair and David aren't playing up and then write up his findings. All thoughts of Lochhead croft and its inhabitants are now completely erased.

***

Winter arrives on October 23rd, a gift from Iceland. A ferocious wind screams across the village for two days and nights, driving horizontal rain ahead, drenching in seconds anyone foolish enough to be outside. The temperature plummets and on the morning of the third day a thin layer of snow covers the houses and the hills. The sky barely lightens, holding a sickly tinge and threatening more snow.

At the new Centre of Highland Wildlife all work has come to a standstill. The bungalow being built for the new Director and his family is finished but not yet ready to inhabit. John is impatient to move and has slept there a couple of odd nights in a sleeping bag with an electric fire for warmth to get the feel of the place. He is finding it more difficult to hide his own problems from Mary and the boys. A week ago he was called away to Edinburgh by his solicitor, as Kate was refusing to agree the proposed financial settlement of the separation and was now asking for, no, demanding, a divorce. The girls had seemed unresponsive and too quiet. When his new home is finally ready he'll have them stay for a while perhaps even Christmas and then he'll try and reconnect. John feels as if he is on a boat drifting helplessly away from the shore. Perhaps it had been a mistake coming here. Should he have stayed with his position at the University and fought Kate harder? But this job is a positive move forward for him and just what he needs right now when he is feeling a failure, less of a man than he was.

Kate's rejection has hurt him deeply, but yet it is more the idea of rejection than a real loss. Sadly, he has stopped loving his wife after several years of her liaisons. Now he is afraid of losing his girls. Outside the wind has diminished and the air seems clearer. On an impulse John picks up his binoculars and his jacket and leaves the Centre. His jeep will get to the back track of the Ben and if the going is OK he'll climb just a little. He's not been there for a while now. The sharp air against his face is good as he gets out of the vehicle. He lifts his head and his nostrils flare as he breathes in. He strides away eagerly. Thank God he's chosen this outdoor life he thinks. For even though the new job will involve more administration than he'd like he knows he'll be able to walk the hills and woods and often climb the Ben.

His head clears and the misery of his domestic life recedes. He'll not go far, just so he can get his records up-to-date, just an hour or so before the light changes. Really he is hoping to see a Snow Bunting blown in from Iceland as one or two were spotted last year, or perhaps a mountain hare. He ascends through pine forest alert for a rare glimpse of a Scottish crossbill and up the steeper path. All these paths will be way marked at the end of winter and observation posts and information boards erected. Behind and over to the southeast stretches an area of moorland with some patches of heather visible even through the dusting of snow where the drainage is good. Juniper and crowberry grow here, as well as alpine club moss and deer grass. John is feeling more positive. He will make a success of his appointment. There is so much he can bring to it; a hands-on approach at the Visitor Centre, a sculpture trail, low-level and upland walks, a guided journey through different climatic zones, bog exploration, fossil history, bird walks, small mammal displays... his mind is racing, competitions for the kids... his pace quickens and his boots follow the westward track across the Ben towards the sea-facing steeper elevations.

At first, John doesn't notice the subtle change in the weather. From being fairly settled, a long moaning wind is snaking round his legs, lifting leaves and stirring grasses. The western sky, which ought to be turning pink now, has a leaden look. It is as if every living creature has gone to ground. The wind increases tugging at his hood, and flecks of white like bits of pale confetti flutter about. Annoyed with himself, John now realizes that he is in the path of an oncoming storm and he needs to get off the mountain as quickly as he can. In an astonishingly short space of time the light shrinks away and it is only experience and knowledge which guide his feet down and around and down again. What little light there is in the sky is being reflected off the loch below, enough to cast the Lochhead croft into darker focus. Rain now hits his face from nowhere, cold smacks of water at first then all too quickly a torrent of icy wetness, which blinds and bites. His feet slither on the wet ground and small rocks roll under his boots. The wind is increasing in strength and John has to bend over to protect his face and prevent himself from being knocked over. Air is trapped inside his over-trousers and they blow out giving him a clownish appearance. Cursing his lack of attention and due care,what kind of example is he as new Director, he'll be a laughing stock, the man stumbles on and then suddenly and swiftly a mountain hare dashes across his track and in an unguarded moment he swerves, slips and crashes to the ground. His head hits a rock and like a chain-sawed pine in the forest he rolls over and lies still.

Rain now turns to sleet. Soon, as the late afternoon temperature falls, it will turn to snow and a blizzard will have its time of power, raging over the mountains and dumping a foot or more in the village below.

The man is felled. He lies across the track, his face upwards towards the swirling sky. His eyes are closed. His hands are curled slightly and a slow trickle of blood is sliding down his cheek, a vermilion gash vivid in the falling whiteness. Then a low groan, a slight movement. The man tries to sit up but he has a thudding pain in his head and his right foot feels strange. But he must move, he must move now and somehow he has to get off the Ben, even if he has to crawl down. He will not survive a night here in these conditions.

***

Alice Brooks has lived alone for a long time. Since she was twenty-five years old twenty years ago, she has always been alone, no matter how many people she lived amongst. She likes it this way. People talk about not having the capacity for commitment in those who choose solitude, when perhaps it is more a fear of dependency, for oneself needing others, and them needing us. Dependency weakens; it brings anxiety, forces compromise and creates fear of loss, whereas commitment is positive, productive and energizing. Relationships ebb and flow and sometimes dry up altogether but work you are personally committed to-that gives your life meaning. Out here, by the loch side, Alice has all she needs and can desire. She is satisfied in so far as it will ever be possible for her to be so, given her past experiences. She doesn't seek happiness for it is unreliable. This is a period of unusual contentment in her life, for a while at any rate, for who knows what will come? Whatever does can't be as bad as what has been. She is grateful for what she has now. So on this wild night the red-haired woman in Lochhead croft stirs the thick vegetable soup she has made for her supper and listens to the wind howling and the steel hawsers, which hold down the corners of the roof into the ground, vibrate and thrum, and feels at peace.

An unexpected bang on the cottage door makes her

jump. It seems at first like something the wind has sent flying, but then another thud and another, too regular for gusts of wind to have created and so comes the surprising realization that someone is at the door. She has not seen any flash of car headlights approaching the cottage, for the window shutters are not quite closed and this would have given warning. So what on earth would any person be doing out in this blizzard on foot? You and I might feel afraid now, alone, defenceless in the troubled dark. Old fears might be stirred in our memories; the stranger outside the door may wish to do us harm. But Alice doesn't feel these kinds of fears. Doesn't care any more about danger. So wiping her hands dry she opens the door.

John has somehow dragged himself off the mountain and hauled his body to the cottage. The faint warm light from a window has given him hope of refuge but his strength is spent and his body chatters and trembles with the effort of reaching it. When the door opens he almost falls in and has to grab hold of the doorframe to prevent himself collapsing. Recovering his balance he staggers forward. Without a word Alice bangs shut the door behind him and stands back to scrutinise her visitor.

What does she see? The man is leaning against a chair for support but she knows his usual strength and fitness for she recognizes him as the ranger from the Centre. She has watched him previously whilst unobserved as he has tracked his way around the hills with his binoculars and backpack, always moving with confidence. Now his face is rough-weathered and pained and blood is still trickling from a gash which is congealing in the brown curly hair above his left ear. He is thoroughly wet and a small pool is collecting beneath his boots and he is agitated.

"Miss Brooks? I'm John Stewart, the new director of the Centre in the village. I'm afraid I've got myself into a scrape on the Ben and…"

"Mr. Stewart, I know who you are. Sit down before you fall over." She speaks quickly but with authority. John does as he is told but even through the exhaustion and embarrassment his brain is struggling to process information.

The woman is dressed in black trousers and a thick Aran sweater, creamy in colour, which emphasizes the redness of her spiky hair. Even so he can see silvery streaks threading through it and at close quarters she seems older than when he had seen her at the loch side from the Ben; possibly she is nearer fifty than forty but then he is not good at estimating ages. His wife is forty and seems much younger. The woman's body is lean, a little too thin perhaps, but she stands tall and her gaze is focused and clear.

He is startled too by the brightness and colour of the croft kitchen. The black range has been cleaned and polished and a blazing fire in the open grate is cheery. There is a vibrant blue and orange rug on the stone floor and a tangerine woven cloth adorns the window shutters. A scrubbed table, two chairs and a rocker stand in the middle of the room and there is a large dresser with some white china, a copper jug and a table lamp. Against the wall is a cupboard with hand painted leaves trailing over it, a fridge, cooker and sink. But the most surprising and arresting feature is a tapestry hanging from a gnarled length of driftwood against a bright white wall. It is entitled 'The Mothers' but is of a group of tall hills of terracotta and vermilion rock rising steeply and set against a cobalt sky. The rocks lean towards each other protectively.

Altogether the effect on John's dazed mind is quite uplifting, He feels as if he has stepped out of a malevolent world into a sanctuary of warmth and colour. Despite his weariness he experiences a surge of relief and a deep gratitude that he is alive.

He takes deep breaths. "I'm sorry to trouble you really, but I think I've twisted my right foot it is swelling and very painful. I'll not make it back to my jeep-it's parked on the east side of the Ben…"

Alice turns away without comment and leaves the room. He can hear the blizzard outside and a humming sound, which rises and falls a little. In a short time she returns carrying a bowl, some bottles and cloths. She pours warm water into the bowl and carefully shakes one or two drops of liquid from two of the bottles. She does all this with total concentration almost as if he is not there and when she is satisfied about her task she turns and approaches him.

"I'm going to clean your head wound Mr. Stewart and then I'll look at your foot. I'm no medic but I may be able to help." The solution smells pleasant antiseptic and sweet.

"What are you using?"

"Lavender oil and witch hazel." Her voice has a mellow tone. Her reply is brief, and she continues to bathe his head, patting it dry and giving him a dressing wad to hold against it. He can sense a taut

21

energy as she leans over him and feels the warmth of her body.

She drags a chair nearer and asks him to put his foot on it. She unlaces the boot and with difficulty pulls it off he leans forward to help but she tells him to sit back. She speaks with an authority he is compelled to obey. His ankle is now swelling rapidly. She removes the sock and reveals the intimately naked red foot. Carefully, tenderly almost, Alice feels all around the ankle, rotating it slowly. Then she tugs each of the toes and bends the foot up and down, and finally turns it from side to side. Her hands are cool with long fingers. It is a strange experience, the man's foot and the woman's hands, nakedly together in this silent encounter. He winces at the pain.

"I don't think it's broken but you've probably got a bad sprain, best to get it checked. If it's possible I'll try to reduce the swelling," and she fetches a large bowl of icy-cold water from the kitchen tap. John shudders as he places his foot in it.

"Leave it there for as long as you can stand it. I'll get a towel. Can you take the other boot off and your jacket and over trousers?" She brings the towel, refuels the fire and fills the kettle.

The evening is drawing on. The woman sits in the rocking chair and assesses the situation. John has fallen silent. He doesn't know what to say, instinctively recognizing that small talk will not do. The fire crackles and sparks and settles itself. Outside the wind is complaining and the waters in the loch are crashing against the shore.

"You'll not be able to get back to your jeep tonight I'm afraid Mr. Stewart."

"Please call me John."

"I can offer you the sofa in the sitting room and perhaps my van will get you out in the morning". Just then the lights flicker and go out.

"That's the power lines down," he says.

This is really awkward. The light from the fire illuminates her pale face. Alice gets up, and goes to a cupboard for a box of candles and methodically places them in jars about the kitchen.

"I've soup and bread and cheese. Should you like some of that?"

He nods. "You're very kind, Miss Brooks." She smiles; "Alice." she says. It all seems a little strange sitting in the half light, isolated from the world, being so polite and perhaps they both sense it is so and the tension relaxes.

John is wiping his foot dry. The swelling has reduced and the pain is numbed by the cold. A dry towel is fetched.

"I've no socks that would fit." So, he wraps his foot in the towel and she hangs his wet things on a rail near the range.

"There now, your new home for a few hours." He is instantly moved by these words and her equilibrium, and fights back a sensation of tears. Home. He hasn't felt at home anywhere for a long time.

Alice directs him to the bathroom that he may clean himself up and whilst he is doing this she makes a fire in the sitting room stove to provide some light and warmth for later.

The soup is heated on the range and supper is eaten. A little conversation takes place, John mainly talking about his new job. She listens well and occasionally asks a question showing perspicacity. The soup is hot and good and with the cheese there are plain scones too. The food and warmth are making him sleepy and when she has briskly cleared away the used dishes, he decides to retire.

The sitting room faces west and south but now large shutters are closed against the view and the wind batters harder here. The firelight reveals other striking wall hangings but he can't quite make them out. He is soon sinking into the warmth of the blankets she has put out for him. From the kitchen come sounds of dishes being washed and put away and the fire being banked up for the night with peat and then, quietness. John lies still, listening. He can only discern sounds from outside. His head is throbbing a little and his foot aches but soon weariness sweeps over him and he falls asleep. His dreams are busy and disturbing. One is about the same mountain hare which had jolted him on the Ben. It had very pale fur and had returned to stare at him as he lay on the ground. Its eyes had been a soft grey which watched him unblinkingly for a long time. Eventually the creature lolloped away and the man had experienced a deep sadness when it left.

At some point during the night the wind had eased off and so it is that John is woken by noises from the kitchen next door. Vivid outlines of light around the shutters tell of morning and so he rises and opens them to allow a thin but clear light to enter the room. Westwards, stretching back to the open sea, the waters of the loch are dark and only a little ruffled. South, he can see the head of the loch and a small

24

wooden jetty that must have been where he had seen Alice enter the water. Anxiously he looks to see if she is out there again but as sounds continue from the kitchen, he realizes she is not. A white coating of snow lies everywhere obliterating the edges of the tarmacked lane. All is serene and beautiful.

He turns and sees the sitting room in all its colour. The wall hangings of woven fabric hang from rails on the north and east walls. One shows a group of children playing on a beach, set against a mazarine sea. The colours are a glorious blend of turquoise, apricot and gold. The other, a long and narrow tapestry, is of a naked woman dancing against a background of vibrant green hills. Her arms reach out to the sky in an attitude of joy but the figure is thin and lithe with small breasts. There is a shock of red hair and John recognizes her, Alice, the woman who is next door preparing breakfast. He feels as if he is intruding on her privacy. The intimacies of the tapestries touch him. He is also amazed. What treasure there is here in the old grey croft which no one visits!

He enters her kitchen and is greeted with a smile. She points to the table. There is a loaf, butter, cheese and honey. She is about to fry some eggs on the range, now hot again from the revived fire.

"Fried eggs OK?" she asks. He nods. "Coffee?"

"Yes, thank you, I'd like that.

"How is your foot this morning?" She brings him the dry socks. "Let me see." Obediently he lifts the injured foot onto a chair. "It's still a little puffy, but better than last night. Can you bear all your weight on it?"

John tries and grimaces a little. It is indeed better but it's going to take a few days to mend. His head has stopped aching.

"I think I'll be able to drive you back to your jeep but do you think you are able to drive yourself back to the Centre?"

It is agreed and so after breakfast Alice and he trudge around to the side of the croft to her van and they wipe away the layer of snow on its windscreen and windows. Cautiously, she moves forward down the lane, and as they leave John looks into the wing mirror to see the cottage recede and something inexplicable in him is full of regrets.

***

Now the light has gone by 3 o'clock and for half the day all life in the village is shut behind closed doors. A few dried leaves flick over the road and dogs bark when anyone walks by. Mary is on a late shift in the village store and is anxious, for the boys will be home from school shortly and on their own. It's not as if they aren't old enough, David is now 10 and Alistair coming up to 13 but they seem to be less sensible these days. Only last week when the power was off in the blizzard David had nearly set fire to the kitchen by messing about with candles and Alistair had just laughed. If she hadn't been home, who knows what might have happened. This time Mary had really been angry, rousing herself from the grey cloud of depression which seemed always to muffle her somehow since Donald's death. David had seemed suitably chastened but Alistair wore a sullen look she hadn't liked.

"You're the man of the house now," she'd told

26

him, hoping this adult role would buck him up. "You ought to be looking after David and me, not playing silly beggars. You should have known better."

Alistair hadn't said a word but stomped off to the bedroom. He was uncommunicative and uncooperative for days after. Ah well. What could she do? With Donald gone the money had shrunk to basic necessities only. She was lucky to top up the income with part-time work in the shop, despite some out-of-school hours. It had been good when John was around but now he'd moved into the new bungalow near the Centre and was busy with his work and furnishing his new home. Mary wondered when Kate and the girls would come. Something was wrong there, she knew, for why was he buying new furniture? And they'd only visited the village once since John had taken the job and he rarely seemed to go to them in Edinburgh. Everything is upset for Mary and she feels as if she is standing on shifting sands.

Just then the shop bell announces a customer and in comes Jennie McLeod, the postie, who lives at the lane end just outside the village.

"Hello, Mary, and how are you today?" Jennie is usually brisk and polite. Her husband is one of the few remaining fishermen coming from a long tradition of men at sea. They have no children for their only son, Jamie, was killed in a road accident when he was two years old.

"Och, not so bad thank you Jennie. What can I get you?" Although the store is self-service she likes to be helpful.

"I've an order for Miss Brooks at the Lochhead croft, Mary. Can I leave it with you to box up and call back in an hour? I can drop it in on my way home but I need to see Rachael McMillan about the Christmas service."

"My goodness, Jennie! It's only just November and you're thinking of Christmas already?" And Mary tries to suppress her dread of this first Christmas without Donald and the anniversary of his death a few weeks after.

"Aye, Rachael is planning some sort of tableaux involving the children this year and I said I'd help. It'll need a lot of preparation I'm thinking."

Rachael McMillan is the Minister's wife and teaches part- time in the local school. Not everyone in the village appreciates her enthusiasm and innovation! Some folk mutter darkly and refer to the old ways.

"That's fine, Jennie. Leave the list with me. How is Miss Brooks doing by the way? Did she cope in the power cut? Three days was quite a stretch, and her on her own."

"Oh, she's a coper, Mary. A strong one that. I like her." It's unusual for Jennie McLeod to be so frank but she has found the woman at the old croft (who must be only a few years older than herself) to be considerate and friendly towards her. Folk in the village have always been carefully respectful and distant, closing down on her after Jamie's death 20 years ago, just when she'd needed company most and Murdo was taking himself off to sea as often as he could. They blamed her she felt for neglect of her boy and indeed, in her heart she has always nursed a fear that such is the truth. So Jennie enjoys her weekly trip to the croft cottage to deliver supplies and tries to allow some time to spare, for she is occasionally invited in for a cup of tea, but what she is discovering about Alice Brooks she keeps to herself.

John has taken possession of his new home. It is a relief now that he doesn't have to stay with his sister, but he feels a little guilty about this, knowing that the boys could do with a man around them. He thinks of his own children, Kirsty and Claire, similar ages to their cousins. Will Kate bring them for Christmas as she has asked? She was quieter than usual with him last time he spoke on the phone. Perhaps the row at the solicitor's office had been a step too far? He shrugs. He's fed up with being pushed around by her. He's his own man now, has a good position and one he is well suited to. Lecturing in the Department of Environmental Sciences brought a reasonable wage but he'd never really cared for the work preferring to be outdoors and therefore is determined not to let the administrative side of directing the new Centre dominate his time. It's just that he misses his girls very much.

With these thoughts in his head, John has gone back out on the Ben. The weather of a week or so ago has changed completely and it is a lovely fresh day, a rare one for November, and he is happy on his own, viewing the village below him. He thinks of the woman at the croft and finds his now-healed foot taking the western path. He is drawn to the place again and is trying to think of a way to thank her for her help and hospitality, any excuse in fact, to visit her again. From the hillside he scans the sky with his binoculars, looking for buzzards, then lowering them he sights the croft house. From up here it looks deserted but he can see the little blue van parked at the side and there is smoke coming from the chimney stack. She is at home then. He focuses more closely on the building, zooming in as far as possible, and can see that the large window on the extended part on the eastern side is uncovered and inside can make out a huge loom. So, this is where she works. The window, facing south, would give good light. He moves his binoculars a little to the left. The kitchen shutters are also open but he can't see Alice at all.

The loch waters are a deep teal colour, rippling rhythmically in the breeze. It is an amazing day, the sky a cerulean blue with pure white clouds and a clarity of light not often to be seen at this time of year. He relishes the cool air on his face and about his head. A day to enjoy. Such a thought makes him start. Perhaps she is out on the lower part of the Ben and has seen him spying? He looks about him, surely he is alone? But now he is unsettled, and so retreats, returning to his jeep via the same route. Why is he defensive?

When John gets home, his new home now, he makes some tea and stands in the kitchen thinking. The bungalow is freshly painted and all its walls are white but yet in the northern light more often than not appear to be grey. He hasn't thought about it before but the experience of bright colour in Alice's home has affected him. He's already bought a bed and linen and a kitchen table. In the sitting room there is a second-hand sofa he found in Fort William but it is dark brown. His place feels gloomy, and then it comes to him, in a flash, the excuse he's been looking for to visit the woman again. He'll ask her advice about decorating his house! This thought that he can legitimately go to the cottage again excites him. He'll take her some logs too as a thank you, he'll saw some tomorrow.

Just then his phone rings and flags up Kate's number. What does she want?

"John, it's Kate." Her voice is tentative, without the strident tone he is used to hearing these days. "Is it alright to talk now?"

He is bemused. She is not normally so considerate of his convenience.

"Yes, I'm at home." It's the first time he has spoken the word 'home' as a separate place and it serves to underline their separation as a couple.

"I'm wondering if the girls and I can come up for a few days. It won't hurt them to miss a day or so off school."

"Are the girls OK?" He wonders why she suddenly wants to visit and immediately imagines there is a problem.

"They're alright John, at least there is nothing obviously the matter. They'd like to see where you are living, that's all." But John suspects that this is not all there is to it.

"I've no beds for them yet Kate. The place is virtually empty. Can't it wait a bit?"

"Well, I've sort of promised them we'd visit this weekend, we can bring sleeping bags, you have central heating don't you?" Her tone is part wheedling and part determined. She is skilled at manipulation but John is becoming more resistant.

"It'll be better to wait Kate. By Christmas, it'll be ready then." And then you'll be free to be with your latest lover he thinks bitterly.

"I really think the girls need to see you sooner than that John. Claire was upset yesterday and I have to talk to you about things. We'll manage, I'm sure."

So John acquiesces for he has a longing to see his children They can spend some time at his sister's perhaps, she'll have the TV and David and Alistair will be company for them. He'll go into the village this evening and arrange something and thinks he'd better get more food in. And so it is that his plans to saw wood and visit Alice are laid to one side.

Several days go by and then the family arrives. "Daddy, daddy!" Kirsty and Claire are rushing towards him and John scoops them up together and swings them round, their legs off the ground and swaying loosely. He pushes his face against their soft hair and smells their fresh girl scents. He crouches down to be at their level and gives each a kiss and a hug. He has missed them too much.

Kate is watching it all; standing by her car she is waiting for him to acknowledge her. She is shapely, has a good figure and has dressed carefully, casual in beige trousers and a scarlet sweater that enhances her full bosom and trim waist. Her blonde-brown hair is cut in a fashionable layered style and she is wearing blusher and red lipstick. In short, she is a modern city woman and stands out here where clothes are chosen for warmth, durability and darkness, so as not to show the dirt. Despite a long drive, she is alert.

"Hello John." She knows she is attractive, and wishes him to notice this, so remains a little at a distance so he can see and admire her figure clearly. John stands up holding each girl by the hand and takes in the well-groomed appearance of his wife. What does he feel? This is the woman who has consistently found him wanting yet is always trying to attract him. Is this her nature? Always needing to be admired and pursued, always needing to be desired? He is a fine looking man, in his prime now, well set with strong features. His unruly head of hair speaks of the outdoors and a certain roughness, which other men can relate to and women find appealing.

The family goes into the new bungalow which is quickly viewed and approved of for its spaciousness and modern fittings. They drink tea and squash and eat the ham rolls he has provided. Tonight they will have supper at the village pub.

At her home Mary bustles around them all, laying out cups and plates and inviting the girls to open packets of biscuits whilst David and Alistair overcome their bashfulness at having their cousins to tea. It's been a while since they were all together and after the tea is taken the children are clamouring to go out. The village has a lighted sports field and a play area with swings and slides and a challenging climbing frame.

The house is suddenly quiet. Mary refills the teapot and slices some more gingerbread and the three of them sit around the fire. Mary is conscious of her drab appearance having dressed as she normally does in an old tweed skirt and dark olive jumper. She doesn't wear make-up, village women of her age hereabouts don't and what would she do that for anyway? Donald wouldn't have liked it. Her clothes feel loose and lumpy or is that how her body feels? Her hair, curly like her brother's, is tangled and grey now. And there sits Kate, fresh and pretty and looks as if she has never had her hands in the sink, or cleared out fire grates or dug up vegetables.

She gets up and pokes the fire.

"Do you like your new home, Kate?"

This question is somewhat spiteful for Mary suspects that Kate and John are not occupying the property together. She is angry with her, the decorative and manicured city woman whose presence seems to mock her own difficult life. What more could Kate wish for? A fine man like her brother, decent, hard working, responsible and good-looking. And there she is herself, her man dead and gone and a lifetime of loneliness when her boys move away. Can't she bear to give up the fine city ways and follow her man, as she should do wherever his work takes him? Isn't this place good enough for her, being too much of a backwater with no slick entertainments and elegant shops? Yet it can be a good life if you made it so. Simple and honest, hard maybe when the weather drew in for days or weeks at a time, but the folk here would look out for you when troubles come. Och, the woman's too lazy and selfish but nonetheless Mary is disturbed by a sense of envy.

"It's fine house, Mary, I like it well." Kate has picked up on her sister-in-law's anger. She recognizes the difference between the new and roomy bungalow and this old, cramped terrace. They live like moles in the winter she thinks and shudders at the thought of herself living so. The conversation is awkward. Questions are asked about the children and the schools, Mary not sharing her concerns that Alistair especially is struggling at school and Kate hiding the fact that Claire is overly tearful of late. The two related women sit within a yard of each other yet are miles apart. Kate is waiting for a chance to speak to John alone and the opportunity arises when he suggests walking around to join the children, for he is keen to spend as much time as he can with his girls. Mary decides to stay behind and Kate does not offer to help wash the dishes.

As they walk down the street, Kate begins.

"I'm having second thoughts John about our situation." He looks about him, hoping nobody has heard her speak.

"The girls aren't coping too well, and perhaps for their sakes we should try again." He is bitter. She makes it sound as if he has never tried, that it's his idea to separate and where is this new concern for their daughters coming from, it was never there when she'd spend a night away, giving her lies about staying with an old school friend who was ill and needed her. And when was she ever interested in his work and his need for a new career in the country?

"Has your latest dumped you then?" It is said harshly but he feels like hurting her.

Kate is silent. She has indeed been dumped and has been hurt enough. John was ever the man to live his own life, putting his work first, leaving to her all the domestic arrangements, unaware that she could have a good career of her own. He's not even been man enough to fight for her.

"The house is good, John. There'll be more space for the girls than in the flat, they'll have a room each of their own they need that at their age and maybe a country life will be good for them. We can keep the flat on for weekend breaks, or perhaps rent it out at holiday times or for the Festival, you can make a fortune then, it would pay for itself."

So that's the game, John thinks cynically. A city love nest for when she gets bored, and freedom from her responsibilities as a mother, for she'd not be taking the children to Edinburgh with her.

"I don't know Kate. It's gone too far maybe this time." And he strides forward to greet the children.

Later that evening as they sit together like any normal happy family choosing from the pub menu, both Kate and John are thinking. He can only do this by being quiet but yet she can still impress Malcolm behind the bar with her charm and figure. He is much taken with Kate, aware of her full breasts and expensive perfume as she leans forward ever so slightly to speak to him in that one-to-one knack she has. Malcolm glances over to where Margaret, his wife, is glowering as she serves drinks.

"Where are Calum and Gordon?" she snaps," I can't do bar work and serve food at the same time." The bar is busy tonight but that's not what is bothering her. As if in reply the loud curses of Calum can be heard from the back room where he is losing a game of darts.

"Go and get them in here" she orders, and Malcolm reluctantly leaves his vantage point.

That night, Kate helps the girls arrange their sleeping bags in one of the bedrooms and herself takes the bed whilst her husband claims the sofa hoping his children don't realize their parent's sleeping arrangements. He lies awake for long time.

The following day is dry and the family drive

down the coast. A shopping centre in Kilsnaig is open and two beds are ordered for Kirsty and Claire, and they choose new duvet covers as a treat. Kirsty selects bright green stripes and Claire a pink, flowery pattern and John remembers his plan to talk to Alice about colours for the walls. How can he do that now?

As they drive back to the village a blue van slows down on a bend going in the other direction. With a jump he realizes that the driver is the very person he has just been thinking about. Alice looks across and recognizes him, and clearly takes in the woman beside him and the two excited girls in the back.

"I know her!" Kate exclaims, "I've seen her face recently in the Scotsman or in a magazine, or something. Now why was that?"

***

Kate has returned to Edinburgh with the children, the matter of reconciliation between herself and John remaining unresolved. He is now busy choosing fittings for the shop at the Visitor Centre and yet from time to time his thoughts are pulled back to Alice and the croft house. He isn't sure why this is so and tries to tell himself that his own wife is more desirable, his own family more important.

One Thursday morning Jim McDonald, one of the Centre's trustees comes to see him.

"Good morning, Mr. Stewart. You're busy I see. Can you spare a few minutes just now?"

The men go into the office and John makes coffee. "What can I do for you, Mr. McDonald?" Mr. McDonald has some unusual news. Old Mrs. Patterson at Am Tealish house has been to see him. She has gifted the new centre a substantial sum of money, £8k in fact, to fund a piece of artwork and had originally thought of a sculpture for the entrance hall. But in talking with Jennie McLeod who delivers her post and is always kind enough to stop for a while to speak with her, she gathers that the woman who came to live at Lochhead croft is an accomplished artist herself. Now Esther Patterson has strong views about supporting local enterprises and has in truth been a prime mover and vociferous advocate for the new centre itself. She thinks now a woven tapestry would make a fine exhibit for the visitor centre's main wall, which faces the glass entrance. Would John visit Miss Brooks to discuss the commission and, if it is accepted, perhaps investigate possible subjects for the tapestry with her?

John's heart answers before his brain. Yes, indeed, he will be happy to do this, what a generous gift from Esther Patterson: he will arrange a meeting as soon as possible.

"Mrs Patterson herself will want to be kept informed and perhaps it would be appropriate to involve her with any design ideas?" Jim McDonald is a considerate and gracious man. Now John has a reason, an excellent reason for visiting Alice Brooks and sends a message via the postie describing the enterprise and requesting a meeting at her convenience.

A few days pass during which John feels unusually invigorated and optimistic and eventually he receives a reply that the following Monday would suit. The morning arrives, grey and soggy, but this time John can approach the croft house without feeling he ought not to be there. She opens the door as soon as he climbs down from the jeep.

"Hello again Mr. Stewart. Do come in out of this dampness." The kitchen is as welcome and cheerful as he remembers and Alice just as centered as before. Today she is wearing a thick embroidered tunic in colours of jade and red over dark straight trousers, giving her the hue of a kingfisher. Coffee is made and John tells her of the proffered commission.

Alice is thoughtful. Finally, she speaks.

"I feel it is an honour to be asked to do this and I accept it gladly. However, (and here she pauses) I have recently accepted a large commission for an arthouse piece for Taos in New Mexico, for one of the museums there. It is going to take me six months at least and I'll need to visit for a couple of weeks. So, I'm looking at next summer, possibly autumn before I can begin anything new."

John thinks this is acceptable and opens up a discussion about possible themes.

"I'd just like to see the Centre to get some ideas about its function, then see the position where the tapestry will hang and of course speak with Mrs Patterson. What an interesting woman she must be!"

John is elated. He will be seeing a lot more of Alice Brooks, in an official capacity too, which will prevent any gossip. After the coffee Alice invites John into her studio to show him samples of weaving textures and colours and a photographic record she has of her work to date. He notices that this begins about nine or ten years ago. The studio is a modern extension to the croft and has a second door leading to a large storage area fully stocked with fibres and wools. The room is dominated by a huge loom, which has been threaded with a myriad of warps. Two smaller looms are pushed against a wall. The south wall of the studio is almost all glass to allow maximum natural light but there are tall folding shutters, painted lilac. The floor is covered with a cream linoleum and the cream walls are covered with photographs of finished pieces and one tapestry, a small but striking hanging in greys and black. It is of an empty prison cell with archetypal iron bars through which a pale blue sky can be seen. In one corner of this is a tiny but brilliantly coloured butterfly. John gazes at this and Alice comes to stand near him.

"This is quite disturbing," he says.

"Not to me," she replies, and turns away. On a wide counter running against two of the walls he sees sketchbooks and swatches of wool threads. Above them is a large board and pinned to it are small images of mountains, plants and birds, not of Scotland but of what he imagines to be New Mexico. The rocks are shades of purple and terracotta rather than grey and there are photos of Native American jewellery, silver and turquoise, heavy and ornate and groups of pueblo Indians staring straight ahead, unsmiling.

"Is this to do with the Taos project?" he asks.

"Yes, I visited two years ago. It's a great place for weaving, lots of tradition in the pueblos, wonderful designs and wools and dyes. I met some interesting people and through them comes this commission. I'm really excited, the landscape is marvellous, desert country with purple sage, wild rosemary and milky blue distant mountains and wide open spaces, free and empty, and amazing art and artifacts. I'm planning a visit in the New Year."

And John feels a stab of envy. Suddenly, he too would like to be going to New Mexico, and with her, and he loves the expression of eagerness in her face.

***

A meeting at the Centre is provisionally arranged for the following Tuesday, with himself, Mr. McDonald and Mrs. Patterson, and John returns to his work. That weekend Kate telephones to say that she will bring the girls for Christmas, and might she also stay too, and could she bring some things for the girls' bedrooms and the kitchen?

Alice decides to meet Mrs. Patterson privately before the visit to the Centre and via Jennie again messages are sent forth and returned. An arrangement is made for a teatime meeting in Mrs. Patterson's rather handsome house. This stands near the Manse in the village and is probably of the same age being a sturdy, stone, double fronted house with bay windows looking out to sea. Money is not in short supply here for Dr.Angus Patterson had been a successful man in Inverness and his wife a chief nursing officer or matron as it was then. The house had been her family home used for holidays when they worked in Inverness. Their sons have long since left home to establish themselves as doctors in England and Esther Patterson now lives alone since Angus' death five years earlier. Her passion, outside of her work, has been with Scottish artists and she has become a patron of a few up and coming young painters, some of whom have exhibited at the renowned Lost Gallery in north-east Scotland, thanks to her efforts. She is quite excited at the prospect of meeting Alice Brooks.

Her contacts in Edinburgh had simply said that she had emerged out of nowhere nine or ten years ago and was already developing an international reputation as most of her work was being commissioned in the Middle East and the United States.

Mrs. Patterson is worried. Perhaps the £8k she has gifted might not be sufficient? Her experience has largely been with painters and sculptors and she knows nothing about tapestries. So this private meeting is fortuitous for it will allow her to raise the matter of finance person to person.

Over Earl Grey tea in fine china cups (Esther abhors the use of mugs) and with freshly made scones and homemade raspberry jam, the two women talk. They like each other immediately. Indeed, it is difficult to dislike Esther Patterson who, despite her age, is a vigorous and kindly person. Both women sense the strength and independence of the other although there is an openness about the older woman not reflected in the younger, who is quieter, more guarded.

The money matter is settled satisfactorily, Esther having been shocked that Alice's Taos commission is in the region of $40,000! But Alice reassures her that she could make a piece she hopes will satisfy for the sum offered, that she regards the invitation as an honour and an opportunity to do something for the place she has made her home.

A very pleasant hour or so passes. As Alice stands to leave she accidentally knocks over the jug of milk and wets her tunic. Esther escorts her to the kitchen to help her sponge this down and as the younger woman rolls up her sleeve Esther's observant eyes notice a network of fine silvery white lines etched into the skin all the way as far as she can see, and knows this for what it isevidence of a long period of self-harming. Alice has become aware of her hostess's observation and briefly the two women gaze into each other's eyes. Nothing is said but the older lady feels both a professional and a motherly concern. This unusual and gifted woman has been unloved.

Some time later, the four persons involved in the project are standing in front of the wall which has been selected as the hanging space for the proposed tapestry. Themes are being discussed and the first idea of a collage of wild life images is passed over as being too obvious and unnecessary considering that the Visitor Centre will contain many such images in the form of photographs.

"What," Alice asks of Esther, "are the themes which interest her?"

"Water, my dear. The sea, the loch, the streams and the rain-all features of this land which have shaped the lives of its people and the creatures and the plants which live here."

The two men nod in agreement but Alice says quietly.

"Water, I'm afraid of water," and John is startled, remembering his sighting of her seeming to disappear beneath the black water of the loch that early morning in September.

They are all silent now until Alice speaks again.

"Yes. I think the idea fits, and it will certainly challenge me. Let me give it some thought and I'll come back to you with some designs. You do know that I can't actually begin until late summer?"

It is all decided upon. Esther and Jim leave and despite John's attempts to keep Alice behind a little longer, she also goes away. He is disappointed, and if the truth be known, a little peeved. Her reserve is not easy to penetrate. What is she really like, this confident, capable woman who seems not to need other people? And why is he so drawn to her?

***

Kate and the girls arrive for Christmas, the car loaded to the maximum with clothing, extra bedding, kitchen equipment, a large rug, books, a small TV (for John hasn't felt the need to have one), seasonal food and gifts. There is also a large framed portrait of Kate, John and the girls taken on holiday by a helpful passer by a really lovely portrait of them all, smiling and relaxed. Kate places it on a window ledge and as she does glances across to her husband. He is wearing a rueful expression.

"We're a good-looking family, aren't we John?" Yes, he thinks, how looks can deceive but he keeps his thoughts to himself. He wants this to be an argument free time so that his girls can enjoy the holiday.

Food is organized and menus planned, and then the family go off to Kilsnaig for last minute present buying. There is an air of anticipation.

A few days before Christmas, they all troop into a packed village hall to watch the Christmas show. The children's tableaux of the Nativity with songs and poems, and a short but delightful dance given by a delicate looking girl destined to go south to the Royal School of Ballet, is truly charming. The audience sing carols lustily and Rachael Macmillan, the Minister's wife, beams. That evening when Kirsty and Claire have gone to bed, Kate and John sit in front of the fire on the new cherry red three- piece suite he has bought after selling the brown sofa.

"I love the colour, John." Kate is stroking the soft pile of the fabric. "It's a jewel colour like ruby. So cheerful. Not a colour I thought you'd choose."

John is quiet. He is thinking of the woman at the croft house. She has gone away, he knows, having been out on the Ben earlier and noticing her shutters were closed and the blue van gone. There was an air of emptiness about the place. He can't help comparing the differences between her and his wife. The one is fierce, strong and beautiful but arresting: the other shapely, slightly blowsy perhaps, certainly pretty, manipulative, he thinks.

"John, I've something to tell you. I've enrolled on a ten week full-time course at the Art Institute in January. It's mainly project management, I.T. and display design. Some conference skills too."

"But what about your job, Kate?" John is worried. This seems so impulsive. Kate has worked as a part-time receptionist at the Grosvenor Hotel for years. He feels that his new salary won't support two homes. Is she doing this to make him go back?

"I've resigned, John. You're not the only one who can change their life, you know! I've enough savings left from mum's legacy to fund the course, though it's not cheap, and to support myself for a while. I'll need to find work after Easter though." She doesn't tell him that she was selected from several others at interview to enrol on the course. She has more pride than he knows.

John is surprised. His wife's diplomas in art and design were obtained a long time ago and new studies now, and the discipline that they would require seem to be a huge step. He had no idea that she wanted a new career for herself. Perhaps separation is her motive now.

"And John," he waits for further revelations, "I've contacted the primary school here and Kilsnaig High and they will take the girls after Easter. Have you thought any more about what I said a few weeks ago?"

"Why do you want to come here, Kate?" he asks this in as much of a civilized voice as he can muster but he's really wanting to cry out I thought you wanted rid of me so that you can pursue other men more easily, and how is a move here going to tie in with a change of career, he is thinking.

Kate looks across at her husband. She sees the hurt and anger, hears the unspoken words. It's a good question. Why does she want to come here and live in this backwater where nobody but the likes of Malcolm at the pub will admire her? Does her own husband actually like her? How much is talked of love and how little of liking. Does she actually like him? For a long time now, probably as long as the children have been around, he has given his best energies to his work, ever conscientious, always occupied. He has given his daughters time and affection, teaching them to observe and classify birds in the city, encouraging them to hike and swim, buying them binoculars and showering them with books and a subscription to RSPB and other wildlife organizations. Yes, he has shared himself with his children. But she herself? Her interests have always been different to his; she enjoys working with people and has skills in bringing out the best in them that her husband knows nothing of. And she has a good eye for design and presentation. She is well liked by staff and guests alike at the Grosvenor Hotel and they are sorry, very sorry, that she is leaving them.

And she must face the truth; she has enjoyed the attention of some lone male guests, has felt flattered and validated somehow by their pursuit of her with expensive meals in city restaurants, visits to cinemas and theatres, and the few sexual encounters that have sometimes followed. But yet, is this the sum total of her worth, an attractive distraction for smart businessmen all most likely married whatever they say? Is she not allowing herself to be used as an ornamental plaything? The last man, Andrew, who has regularly stayed in the hotel, and someone she had hoped might really value her for he was intelligent, interesting and courteous, had talked too much this time about his wife and family in Durham, and then had mentioned in passing that his company was transferring him soon to Nottingham and his area would now be in the Midlands. He had said very politely that it had been nice knowing her, and something in his voice gave that word another meaning, and a cold numb feeling had spread from her stomach throughout her body.

They'd had sex for the last time, discreetly in his hotel room and as he lay on top of her there had been a point when she was fighting back tears. Could she go on like this? Or could she face life alone. Just her and the girls, and eventually just herself? She had

47

loved her husband once and wanted to again but in truth they hardly knew each other.

These were the thoughts in Kate's mind as she struggled to answer John's questions and which now hung in the air between them. And what of another, as yet unasked question? Did he really want her to come and live with him? The spaces between people are as unfordable as a fast flowing river and most often when they are supposed to be closest.

Christmas Eve arrives and they all go to Mary's house for supper and she is all too grateful for their company as this is the first Christmas after Donald's death and the boys are alternately sullen or over feisty. When the cousins settle down to watch a film on TV Mary suggests to John that he and Kate walk to the pub for a drink for she is finding Kate's close proximity difficult still and has her own sadness to deal with.

"I've still to wrap up some gifts and must prepare vegetables for tomorrow, so off you go and enjoy some free time together."

The Lobster Pot is noisy and hot. Kate removes her jacket and makes herself comfortable in the proffered seat that an admiring forestry worker points out. Her blue top is low cut and partly reveals her still firm and generous breasts. Tonight she is wearing a short skirt and high-heeled shoes. Several glances take note of her shapely legs. John is somewhat envied by other males. He returns from the bar and squeezes in beside her. Folk are getting to know him now and he is soon engrossed in conversation. Not to be outdone Kate engages in talk with the couple on her right and is glad to discover that there are quite a few couples in the village of her and John's age with children and that the schools are well thought of. The chilled glass of Chardonnay for her and the pint of bitter for him slip down easily in the over-heated bar lounge. Laughter mounts and John turns to share the discussion his wife is clearly enjoying. His arm drapes over the seat back behind her and he leans inwards to join the group conversation. More drinks are ordered and John relaxes as the alcohol does its work. His hand slips and he keeps it round his wife's waist. Truth be told John rather likes the envy he senses from some of the other men in the bar. They are a handsome couple and there are many who would welcome this new and interesting family to the village. Margaret, behind the bar, is not one of them however. All these outsiders coming in, that strange woman at the croft house who thinks she is above all the locals, never mixing, and this new Centre, all the tourists and city folk tramping over their hills and parking their huge cars where they liked and that man, the new Director and the brand new house and his shiny woman! Others might think that the increase in business for the pub would be welcome but for Margaret this only means more work, as her sons are idle louts she cannot depend on. God help anyone who might point this out though.

John and Kate collect the girls and walk home. It is a clear cold night with a full moon and many brilliant stars. The pavement glitters with a night frost. At home, he pours a whisky whilst Kate says goodnight to the girls. The fire in the log- burning stove is quickly revived, and the bright flames and crimson upholstery give the room a welcoming feel.

"Do you want a night cap Kate," he asks, topping up his glass with a large malt.

"Och, yes please" she mimics and kicks off her shoes, curling up on the sofa, relaxing her body in the warmth.

He sits beside her. The beer and the whisky are unravelling him and all feelings of uncertainty slip away. He feels well and proud of himself and optimistic about his new life here. His wife is very attractive and he can smell her musky perfume and sense the softness of her hair and skin. Kate is relaxed too and sleepy. The Edinburgh flat has no open fire and although comfortable it lacks the primal experience of watching logs spark and blaze when outside the cold night deepens its hold on the land.

"This is lovely, John," she murmurs, and half turns towards him as she speaks and before anything is thought or decided the man and woman are making love before the fire. Afterwards they go upstairs to the marital bed. And so it is on Christmas morning their girls tumble into bed with them, excited and happy, and there is a great flurry of unwrapping of parcels.

The New Year comes with its usual festivities and John and Kate maintain a closer relationship and the children are happy. It is with a little regret that John helps to pack the car when they must return to Edinburgh. The girls don't want to leave either but the time of departure comes and soon the three of them are in the car.

"Oh, I've left my handbag in the kitchen," exclaims Kate and John goes in to retrieve it and trips down the front step on the way back, spilling its contents over the path. As he hastily gathers them up he sees a small photo of a fine-suited man in white shirt and tie, and on the back a message. 'To my special friend, Kate.' A tide of anger sweeps over him. The two-timing bitch and he strides to the car thrusting the bag through the open window and throwing the photo in Kate's face. Kirsty and Claire are alarmed and Claire begins to cry at this sudden and terrible change in her father's manner. Kate is frozen in her seat. What can she say? So slowly, miserably, she puts the car into gear and drives away.

John doesn't see the tears pouring down her cheeks and cannot know the anguish of her feelings, the sense of loss and desolation, uncertainty and fear, but she can imagine his fury and contempt as he bangs shut the front door. Kate battles to drive safely the long journey back to Edinburgh whilst sobbing gently, but must pull in to comfort Claire who has cried broken heartedly and to worry about Kirsty, who stares at her with hostility, for she too has seen the photo and understands more than she ought.

John does what a man of his nature will do in circumstances like this. He climbs into his jeep and drives into the hills, parking the vehicle and climbing the slopes with an energy produced by anger and bitterness. He reaches the summit and stands a lone figure bleakly silhouetted against the sky, unseeing and full of pain. He stands for a long time.

***

A week later Alice comes into the Centre as John is finishing a discussion with a joiner about shelving. She enters so quietly it is a while before he realizes she has been waiting and watching him.

"I'm sorry to disturb you, John." He is pleased

that she has used his Christian name for the first time. "I've been at my loom too long and needed to get out and thought it might be useful to measure the space for the tapestry. Is this a bad time? I can come back."

"Not at all. Dougie and I have just finished. Come into the office for a moment."

Alice can see that something has changed in John. His face seems stiff somehow, as if he is controlling himself. She seems, as ever, a contained but observant person, whose open gaze reveals no obvious emotion but is not unfriendly either. She is wearing a long waterproof coat in a rich rust colour, a pale blue hat and stout walking boots.

"Have you walked here?" he asks, for it is over two miles from her home to the Centre and the day is dreich.

"Yes, I need the exercise and fresh air." And her usually pale skin glows with health.

In the office, John makes hot drinks. He is still smarting about his wife's betrayal and has refused to telephone even to check whether they had arrived home safely as he normally would have done. He cannot bring himself to hear her voice. So, he is indeed a little more formal with Alice, wary, confused about his feelings. He can do without women in his life at the moment, he thinks, and is grateful for his work.

The tapestry area is measured and a note taken and as Alice turns to leave she asks if he has enjoyed the holiday break with his family, for Jennie, the postie, has spoken of their visit over a cup of tea. What can he say?

"Yes, thank you" but spoken a little crisply, a little

hastily, and Alice recognizes that all is not well and for a reason she cannot understand finds herself inviting him to supper, and John, now thoroughly confused, accepts.

An evening is arranged and when the day arrives he dresses himself more carefully than usual, choosing a good shirt and warm jumper. He has purchased a bottle of red wine and then worries in case she prefers white. It is dark when he drives down the track to her home and he is glad that folk in the village won't see him, although he has legitimate business with her, doesn't he? But really the evening is beginning to feel like an assignation so there is an edge of anticipation to it.

Tonight Alice invites him into the sitting room where the log burner glows with heat. He offers the wine and she gracefully accepts and asks whether he would like a glass but when she comes back from the kitchen she is carrying only one glass of wine, her own containing water.

"Do you not like red wine? I wondered whether I should have brought white."

"I don't drink alcohol, John. Haven't done so for nearly twenty-five years."

Is or was she an alcoholic, he wonders? But does not ask. They talk about his work and hers; he is curious about her weaving. When did she begin, where was she trained, where has she lived and so forth? Alice adeptly manages to answer his questions without actually revealing too much about herself. She turns the conversation more towards him and during the meal, a vegetable curry with basmati rice, followed by fruit and cheese, he finds himself telling her about Kate and their marital difficulties.

Alice is a sympathetic listener and John feels a sense of relief as he unburdens himself. She doesn't offer advice, or platitudes, merely listens and with unobtrusive encouragement allows his unhappiness to spill out. By the end of the meal, John feels strangely comforted and as he drives home his thoughts are of wonder about this enigmatic and seemingly wise woman who has come to live amongst them. He decides that he will see her again but doesn't yet know how.

Two days later he is standing in the Lobster Pot with Jim Macdonald. Malcolm is serving the early evening drinkers when his wife Margaret bursts into the room waving a newspaper.

"I told you there was something not right about that woman at Lochhead croft, didn't I? Now I've found her out. It's all in this old copy of The Scotsman. I discovered it when I was cleaning out the boot cupboard. She's only a child murderer, that's what! Come to be here amongst us to hide herself, no doubt. What about our children, they'll no be safe any more? Twenty-two years in Cornton Vale for murdering her own bairn!" And she throws the yellowed newspaper onto the bar counter for all to see and there staring up at them, the unmistakable face of a younger-looking Alice Brooks and beneath the photograph a headline

Edinburgh woman convicted of child murder

Margaret stands, legs apart, her face bulging with wrath, triumphant.

A hand grenade casually tossed into the room could not have created greater commotion than

Margaret's announcement. People push forward to see for themselves the creased image of Alice Brooks staring out at them. John, paralyzed by the news, is thrust aside, and all the while the expression of exultation on Margaret's face reveals her repressed hatred of the woman at Lochhead croft.

Where does this enmity to the stranger originate because without the outsider humanity would stagnate and wither? Why do we humans almost always rejoice in the exposure of another's sin or crime? For it is not just a sense of gratitude or relief that justice has prevailed, justice to make our society safer for us all...it is also a kind of glee in the news of another's downfall.

John Stewart however, feels none of this. After the initial shock comes numbness; a coldness spreads through his body, then the physical sensation of nausea. He leaves the room, staggers to the outside door and gulps down the rain-lashing air. His legs are shaking and he is aware of a contraction round his chest; his lungs can't seem to get enough oxygen.

Can this be true? Is there some dreadful mistake? Is the woman he has recently eaten supper with and opened his innermost feelings to, really a person who could kill her own child? His brain cannot process the news, cannot relate the two kinds of women this revelation has created. He finds his vehicle and shakily starts the engine. In a daze he drives home where he quickly pours out a large whisky. The deep warmth of the drink revives him a little and he sits down to think. He decides she owes him an explanation. After all he has trusted her, they all have, Jim McDonald, Esther Patterson, Jennie McLeod...

his feelings range from anger to confusion. How could she possibly be a murderess ... her recent kindness to him, her courtesy, her hospitality, and yet it is true she is reserved, private, perhaps even secretive. What has she been hiding from them?

She has made little effort to belong to the community, has kept herself aloof, unknown, organizing private deliveries of food and fuel ... And her not drinking alcohol, her vegetarianism, her flamboyant clothes ... all seem now to mock the ways of the village. Her confidence arrogance some might say her self containment all now can be seen as a rejection of the whole community.

John takes another large measure of whisky. He feels personally betrayed. First his wife, then this woman who has somehow enticed him, almost befriended him, but because of this sordid secret now has somehow diminished his embryonic relationship with her. For how can he possibly continue a friendship with her if this news is true? Surely, she will now be exiled from all life in the community. Esther Patterson will withdraw her generous commission; the village shop will decline her deliveries of provisions. The woman will have to leave.

Desolation sweeps over him, for John now understands the loneliness of his own situation.

The whisky takes effect and sleep creeps over him. It is cold in the sitting room when he wakes and his very first thoughts reflect the goodness of his nature for he thinks of her, Alice, alone at the croft house, as yet unknowing that her history has been made public. Suddenly recalling that look of malignant satisfaction on Margaret's face, he fears for her. So quickly, he drives away from his home and towards the loch. It is late and very dark. The rain is driving down hard, nobody is about and from the road he cannot see lights at the croft house. She will be in bed he thinks, what should he do? Warn her perhaps. So he drives down the track and then realizes her van is not there. She is away. He feels some relief for truly his emotions are too raw just now. He returns home and tries to sleep. Soon after dawn the following morning, John has a plan. He will find Jennie, the postie, and discover what she knows for he believes that only he and she have been invited into Alice's home. Jennie might know when Alice will be back.

Jennie and Murdo McLeod's cottage is just off the edge of the village where the main road bends and where their son Jamie was knocked down by a builder's truck in 1987. He was just two years old and although it was given at the inquest as accidental death, it became known that Jennie had been watching television and that an opened bottle of sherry had been seen by the women, who sat with her later, and two empty bottles outside. And this in mid-afternoon, not watching her bairn who had wandered into the road. Whatever the truth of this and nobody really knew, an already taciturn Murdo had withdrawn in his own grief away from his wife and no more children were born to them. Jennie had not kept many friends after that. She was the post woman for the village and so knew everyone, and they knew her, but she kept in her cottage outside working hours and didn't much mingle. Only the Minister's wife, Rachel McMillan, had been sympathetic. So when

Alice came to live nearby, who knew nothing of Jennie's history, but who seemed nonetheless to understand her in some way, an attachment was made. Jennie was drawn to the woman, perhaps seeing in the strong independent and skilled weaver the sort of person she herself might have been before she married Murdo. And she alone was permitted inside the croft house to admire weavings and learn about the looms.

So it is to Jennie that John goes that early morning before the village is up and doing, and whilst Murdo is out on the usual four am fishing.

He walks to the postie's house and knocks as quietly as he can, not wishing to wake up curious neighbours. There is a light in the side room and when nobody comes to the door he goes around the back and taps on the window.

Startled, Jennie, in her woollen dressing gown looks up and lets him in.

"Mr. Stewart. Whatever is it brings you here, and this early?" and suddenly she adds, "It's not Murdo is it, has something happened?" She becomes agitated.

"No, no, Mrs. McLeod, not that, not that at all. It's another matter I've come to see you about." And over a mug of tea he tells her the news that probably only a few in the village are now unaware of. Jennie is upset and disbelieving.

"I don't believe a word of it!" and yet, as she speaks, she instinctively knows really the truth of it, knows that in some mysterious way that this is what has drawn her to Alice all along, that they share some awful loss in common.

John tells her about the newspaper photo- he only

knows himself what has been said in the pub the night before and expresses his current concern about the reception that Alice might receive when she returns. He doesn't say why it is his concern and Jennie doesn't ask him.

Does she know when she is coming back? In fact, Jennie does know Alice is meeting someone in Edinburgh, something to do with wools, a new supplier she thinks and Alice should be back tomorrow afternoon. During the day ahead, John keeps to the Centre and tries to focus on his work. The shelving in the storeroom is complete and furniture is being selected. Soon reception staff and an events and educational liaison officer will be needed. An opening event after Easter is being planned. But his efforts are desultory as all the while his thoughts of yesterday's revelation, and his own confused feelings keep occupying his mind.

At 11am Jim McDonald telephones. He has heard the rumours, though he is not a man to give rumours much credence, but what does worry him is news that a group of men, led by Calum and Gordon McKenzie and encouraged by some of the womenfolk, are planning a confrontation with Miss Brooks when she shows up at the croft house. He is off to speak to the Minister to see what can be done.

John is horrified. A vigilante party! Already! A few minutes later, Esther Patterson calls into the Centre. She has heard the news too from Margaret McKenzie, the village shopkeeper and can't believe it. Esther's first response, despite her long experience in the medical world of folks' weaknesses, is usually a generous one. But then, she pauses, remembering those fine silver lines etched into Miss Brooks' arms. There are secrets here, evidence of a troubled mind, but she keeps these thoughts to herself

The day and night are endless. At lunchtime, before the afternoon Alice is due back from Edinburgh, John drives to the crossroads, parks his jeep and waits. He tries to position himself so that he can see any traffic in the mirror but outgoing travellers from the village cannot see him. When a vehicle approaches he pretends to be viewing through his binoculars. He listens and waits. Each time he hears the sound of a car engine he is fully alert, but she doesn't come. Time passes by slowly: he watches the raindrops sliding down the windscreen. The light is starting to fade and then there it is, the blue van in his rear view mirror. He switches on his engine and abruptly cuts her off. She sounds her horn, not recognizing the jeep's erratic driver. Quickly John stops and strides towards her.

"John, is that you? You gave me a scare, jumping in my way like that." But his expression and urgency changes her tone. "What's wrong?"

"They know in the village."

"Know what?"

"An old Scotsman newspaper. Your trial for killing your bairn, plus a photo. They will come after you, some of the men I think. You should follow me we'll take your van to the car park up the Ben road, it's closed so nobody will go there and then you must come back with me."

Without hesitation Alice does as he suggests and follows him away from the main road and up a winding track to the car park in the forest.

"Is it true?" His first words blurt out when they are parked and out of sight. He leans back in the driver's seat as she climbs in next to him.

"I was convicted of killing my little boy Robbie in 1980 and served 15 years in Cornton Vale prison before I got parole." Her voice is steady. Matter of fact. John shivers, he cannot take this in and struggles to process her words.

"You were convicted! So it is true. You killed your own bairn! And he recoils from her. All hope that there has been a ghastly mistake now gone."

"No. I didn't kill him though I confessed to it. I was responsible for his death though so I deserved the conviction," and her tone of voice is sad, utterly sad. She is not offering any justification or argument: she speaks softly and her face seems to age before his eyes.

"They all know in the village. Margaret McKenzie found the old newspaper with your picture, your name on the front page. They are angry and may harm you. It's not safe here.

"I've nowhere to go." She speaks flatly.

"Your parents, family?"

"All dead."

"Then you must come with me. Leave your van here. The car park is officially closed till the spring so nobody comes here. Come back with me now before you are seen." And so as dusk edges out the day, Alice is smothered in blankets in the back of John's jeep as he drives her to his bungalow. The blinds and curtains are closed and the door is locked, and there they stand, facing each other in the sitting room.

PART TWO

What later remained was the woody scent of the wild daffodils as their pale petals and delicate fluted edges of the narrow trumpets fluttered in the warm spring air.

One afternoon they had walked from the cottage through the secluded wood, hand-in-hand, in the softly dappled light, through the new growth of ash and birch trees, the feathery leaves just breaking out and shimmering in the shafts of sunlight. Flickering shadows followed them as if they were being accompanied by wood sprites, glad to be resurrected after the dead of winter by the newly emerging friendship of the human couple.

They hadn't spoken much for the sounds of the secret life of the wood around them was all the conversation needed. Above them, through the whispering tree canopy, ice cream scoops of cumulus clouds hung in a cerulean blue sky. The citrus green leaves of the sprouting shoots pulsated with hard energy. Wood sorrel flowered, creamy white, creeping along the edges of the narrow footpath, and pink water avens were opening out at the vigorous stream's verges. If there were any creatures about they waited, in stillness, watching from behind the shaded safety of foliage, curious perhaps, about the man and the young woman sharing for a while their natural habitat. A brook burbled somewhere out of sight and a blackbird gave its harsh alarm call, clack-aack-aack-aack.

He had brought a rucksack and a tartan patterned

car blanket, which he had laid down in a mossy clearing. From the rucksack he produced his camera and equipment, a bottle of wine and incongruously two beautiful wine glasses. They drank the cool, green-gold Chablis sitting facing each other. He gazed at her for a long time absorbing the exact shade of her orange-red hair, which seemed to spring out of her head, as madder stained as a Martinengo lute. Tendrils of curls framed her face, her skin shining pale in the beams of sunlight falling upon her. She wasn't beautiful in a conventional sense. Her nose bent slightly, one nostril a little wider than the other, and the right eye more oval-shaped than the round left one. A few freckles splattered across her nose and cheeks, randomly, giving her a childlike look, yet her mouth was generous, sensuous, and the teeth were straight and white.

He picked up his camera and began taking pictures. It was what they had come for. He calculated carefully the focal length and exposure time for his purpose. He worked steadily, concentrating fully on the task, like an animal totally engrossed. A little embarrassed, unused to such professional focused attention, she laughed nervously, but he said no, he wanted her to look serious, as she had done when they had first met.

The photographic session continued and then he asked if he could take pictures of her against one of the trees, so she stood and leaned back against the silver-bandaged bark of a birch.

"I would prefer it, if you were naked. Would you mind?" His voice was mellow, engaging, and he smiled just a little, to show her this was OK and normal and not threatening. So, self-consciously, because he was fully clothed and they were outdoors, she did as she was bid, and took off her jeans and jumper and stood, shivering slightly in her bra and briefs.

"These too, please," he pointed at them.

"Why do you want me so?" she queried, unsure of herself.

"I'm putting together a collection of pictures which juxtapose textures it's a favourite theme of mine, so in this instance (and she is not sure she likes that word as it makes her feel temporary) textures of human skin, hair and tree bark. Also the colours will be striking, your creamy skin, the burnt sienna of the tree-bark and its silver bands, and of course the vermillion of your hair."

His language, the words describing the colours as if he were a painter, reassured her, but nonetheless hesitant, she moved away from him and slipped out of her briefs, and unfastened her bra. As she turned towards him, her pointed breasts gleamed in the sun's soft buttery light and the nipples stood out bud-like and pink. She was very slender, willowy amongst the trees. A froth of golden hair marked her crotch, a few tones lighter than the hair on her head. She wrapped her arms around herself for warmth and privacy.

He came over and re-arranged them against the tree-bark, wordlessly, utterly professional, though in truth he was already aroused by her frail beauty. Every now and then, between photographs, he would ask her whether she was all right and would then gently but firmly place her head this way, then that, or move her limbs. Next, he turned her around facing the tree, positioning her arms and legs wide in a tree hug, exposing the long line of her back and the slope of her buttocks and the curve of her waist and hips. The rough wool of his jacket brushed against her skin disturbing her. She felt cold and vulnerable.

When he had finished, satisfied with his work, he came to her at once murmuring thanks in his low English voice and wrapped his jacket around her, then took her in his arms. He kissed her hair, stroked her neck, all the time whispering his thanks, saying that she had been a great model, had done it all superbly, that the photographs would be wonderful, that he would make her famous.

He led her to the blanket and they lay there entwined until warmth restored her. Their lovemaking soon began, the first kisses quickly became hard and insistent, and her initial resistance, born of un-use, of emotional virginity, was slowly broken, and strong surges of unfamiliar sensations welled up inside her. Inhibitions vanished that they were out in the open where anyone walking by could come upon them even added to the rising sense of excitement. His passion inflamed hers; his experience directed her... and only the scent of daffodils and the surge of sap swelling their stems as they swayed in the light breeze remained as an image in her head. She was taken by surprise that her body was capable of such an autonomous response, that it had its own needs, its own life even, like the beginning of life in the trees and plants around her, and the young woman she thought she was had vanished and a new, empowered female had replaced it. Sharp streams of pleasure spread downwards through her groin and into her inner thighs and the climax came urgent and sweet, jolting from her a loud gasp.

Afterwards, lying together, their breathing blending with the natural sounds of the forest, the herbal fragrance of the dancing daffodils wafted over them. He smiled at her and kissed her nose, cheeks and mouth. The smile widened into a wolfish grin and she knew he had planned it all somehow, and this evidence of his male power was pleasing. She dressed and hand in hand again but now with a more intimate connection, they retraced their steps through the softening light to the cottage. Later, much later, Alice Brooks will never have daffodils near her.

***

It's always difficult to know where a story begins or ends. Like life itself, we enter at chapter five and leave before the finish, a feature of our existence, which still astonishes us, and there are so many beginnings and endings. Memory itself is fluid, a remembering of history from changing, current perspectives so that the past ceases to exist except as a construct of our varying imagination.

How then can Alice do justice to her own story? How is John to understand the core experiences of her life which he hasn't shared and which have led her to this moment sitting in his home before the light of a log fire, the wind getting up outside and dark shadows deepening in the village?

"My beautiful Robbie," she almost whispered his name, then her voice changed and became detached. "Robbie died in 1980. He was only four years old, and I was twenty." She stopped, for already she has described, in barely a dozen words, a central huge chunk of her life. "I'd been a wilful, wayward teenager, an only child. My father, James, was a surveyor and my mother, Sarah, worked as a school secretary. I became pregnant with Robbie at a party when I was sixteen. I had to leave school and my parents supported me and my baby in their home. It wasn't easy for them at that time. I continued my studies. I was bright and there had been high expectations of me so I'd been a huge disappointment to everyone when I got pregnant. I was quite fierce though. I think mum had always found me daunting. I was stronger willed than her and always got my own way.

It was an easy birth and I loved my baby, my golden boy. He had hair like mine but lighter with more gold in it and it was always tousled. He hated having it combed. He would sit on my knee and I would use my fingers to disentangle it. He had a smile which lit up the room. Everyone adored him. I was happy just being his mum and staying at home but dad insisted that I studied for my exams.

When I was nineteen I applied for and got a place at Edinburgh University to study textile design and development. Then dad surprised us all; he had taken a lease on a small apartment for me and Robbie halfway between home and university. He would pay the rent and give me a small allowance to live independently. Mum said she would ask for part-time work and help me apply for bursaries and grants and Robbie could spend some time at play school and pre-school and she would look after him when I was at lectures. I had to promise to study in the evenings when Robbie was in bed. My father had figured that I needed to step away from living with him and mum and begin to take some responsibility for myself and my son. It was amazing. They were wonderful. A whole new life was beginning, a second chance, and I was so excited.

I remember that first day at Uni. I walked from my flat Robbie had been collected by mum in her little Fiat and the pavements were glossy after rain. The late September leaves were all shades of gold and red. It was my favourite time of year. I love colour. I think we greatly underestimate its effects upon us all. My heart was skipping light. It was to be the first day of the rest of my life, September 1979.

I soon settled into a pattern: morning lectures, collecting Robbie from mum or playschool, a walk with him to the park or the shops or if there was an afternoon lecture he would stay with mum and we'd eat tea together. Then I would bath him and put him to bed. He loved stories, especially about animals, so this was a favourite time. The hard part was afterwards for I'd have to get out my books and focus on the work knowing that my fellow students were meeting in the Union bars or local pubs and cafes. I missed their frivolity and zest for their freedoms. Most knew I had Robbie but occasionally if I was asked out on date, I had to explain my situation. Gradually, no one asked me any more and I felt a bit excluded.

But Robbie was my beautiful boy. He was growing well, sturdy and amiable, and I enjoyed my studies. I loved textiles and had ambitions to become a weaver. Mum and dad had taken us all to Orkney the previous summer and I'd met a woman who lived on the coast near Brough Head on the Mainland and who wove huge tapestries on enormous looms. I loved her work and wanted to do something similar. My course though was about design and development and as yet, quite theoretical. In the meantime I'd seek out unusual pieces of fabric and wools and loved making simple things for me and Robbie to wear. I made him a cap which he loved so much he'd go to bed in it. It was blue with a tartan edging and a green tassel."

Alice continued her story relating how sometime in December of that first term she became aware of a series of black and white posters around the campus and in the city. Edinburgh was a magnet for the best and most creative of artists and after Christmas there was to be a series of lectures to augment an exhibition of photographs by the already internationally known artist, Henry Wildgoose. His latest work was surrounded by controversy. The images focused on pubescent girls at that Janus stage, caught at the pivot between childhood and womanhood. The photographs were disquieting. Pure, open faces would gaze upon the viewers; large wide eyes and unblemished skin, seemingly childlike and innocent, but the mostly naked bodies would show small breasts and hints of body hair and would be positioned in provocative poses. The pictures were beautiful and unsettling at the same time. But what attracted Alice's attention was the inclusion in all the photos of fabrics and textures furs, rough wools, tweeds, silks, net, sacking, wood and metal, juxtaposed with the soft unblemished skins of the children. This use of textiles and other materials intrigued her and she decided to attend the first lecture to be given on the third

Monday in January at 6pm, even though this meant asking her parents for extra child-minding.

The day before this event was her birthday. She was twenty years old. There was to be a tea party at her parents' home and Robbie had been excited all weekend about this, as he had secretly helped his grandma to make a special pink birthday cake for his mum. Alice was looking forward to the forthcoming lecture but that afternoon James Brooks had expressed his dislike and unease for what he knew of the photographer's work, recalling a review from 'The Scotsman' suggesting that there were those who considered these particular pictures bordered on the pornographic. Alice argued against this saying that the artist was simply and rightly expressing a truth, an uncomfortable one maybe, but it was the artist's job to be unafraid. James and Alice had always been close since he recognized her intelligence and had fostered it. Sarah, however, had ever struggled with the way her daughter thought and behaved, usually bewildered by her impetuous, wilful character, but yet somewhat in awe of the vitality and strength in her only child. She found her easy-going, funny grandchild much easier to manage.

And so it was arranged that Robbie would stay overnight on Mondays with his grandparents so that Alice could attend the series of lectures.

"It was raining and I had to walk as usual, but I was pleased with my appearance for I wore my favourite outfit, orange cord trousers and an acid yellow sweater and a second- hand velvet jacket I'd bought, a lovely rich burnt umber. It was quite noticeable. Do you think John there is an unconscious mind in us, which has its own agenda, planning and making decisions we are not in control of? Or are there unknown forces at work which will be conjured up like malevolent tricksters to uproot our very beings and set us on paths undreamed of in our ideas about ourselves?"

The lecturer began:

"Good evening ladies and gentlemen. I am gratified to see so many of you here for this first in a series of six talks about my work, and in particular my current interest in the ambiguous face of sexuality in young people and its relationship to our unconscious fears and desires. Firstly, I shall project a series of images silently, and then a second showing during which I shall attempt to describe my purpose and methods and answer any questions you may have."

His English voice was fluent and deep with a resonance of once flattened vowels, remnants of a Midland upbringing. The way in which he spoke, his head held high and with alert eyes, gave an impression of a man who knew his capabilities. Alice had read the short biography, which presaged the course details. Born in 1944 that made him at least 35 years old. A man in his prime. He wasn't slender like her. He was sturdy, with a large head and pronounced features, dark brown eyes and an unfashionably half-shaven skull. He looked brutish. His clothes, for Alice automatically noticed what people chose to wear, consisted of grey tweed jacket over a black sweater and trousers which emphasized his appearance to be more like an ordinary working man in his weekend attire than that of an artist, or what she imagined an artist might look like.

If Alice was already assessing Henry Wildgoose, then he had quickly noticed her as she sat at the end of a row of seats about a third of the way down the hall. Her long legs were outstretched and her pale face was in sharp contrast to the amazing richness of her hair and clothing. He marked her out in his mind as one to speak with later.

The meeting was well attended. The images were projected and details given about camera techniques. Just then, however, there was a rumpus from the back of the hall and someone, a man, stood up and shouted.

"Shame on you! Shame on you for exploiting young girls for your own gratification and commercial gain. You should be locked up, not celebrated for these degrading pictures." Everyone turned and stared in that mixture of horror and thrill when disturbances are made. The man was hustled away by staff and Henry Wildgoose was left to respond.

"Ladies and gentlemen. You have heard my critic just now. It is a charge laid against me that I exploit children. First, I must tell you that each subject's parents and always the mother, were present at all times during the shoot, and that they, of course, had given full and written consent for the pictures and poses I made. Secondly, that the very essence of the criticism underpins the points I'm trying to make- namely that it is we ourselves who have difficulties in accepting the natural, powerful sexuality which emerges in us at puberty and this unease in us reflects psychological disturbances about our own sexuality. My work shows how necessary it is for us to examine our own confused feelings and repressed natural responses despite this age of so-called liberation. What frightens us is when we see the naked truth of our human development in these, to me, beautiful images of the process of leaving childhood behind and becoming adults. Perhaps you would care to discuss these matters with me further in the University bar?"

Alice decided to stay for a drink and wondered whether she would get a chance to ask her question privately about his reasons for using fabrics in the photos, but Henry Wildgoose was surrounded by eager students wishing to gain his attention. So she went across the campus to Ricardo's for a coffee and to spend some time with other young people, a rare opportunity for her.

At about 10pm Alice made up her mind to go home for her days began early, and as she was putting on her coat she was surprised to find herself being helped, and turning round realized that Mr. Wildgoose himself was holding her jacket open.

"Hello," he said, "I noticed you in the hall earlier. Did you enjoy the lecture?"Alice was taken aback, especially as his question had been put almost tentatively, modestly.

"Yes, in fact I did. Apart from the interruption that is."

"Ah yes. And what are your views about my exploitation of young people Miss...er?"

"I'm Alice Brooks. I think the pictures are beautiful, but also disturbing. I hadn't thought of myself as being repressed!" She was thinking about her own wild behaviour which had led to Robbie. Her expression was serious and thoughtful and close up he could see more clearly her porcelain skin and the way her lips opened to reveal her neat teeth. Her gaze was direct and frank, but he sensed too some slight anxiety in her body, and in truth. Alice was beginning to feel somewhat nervous. His presence affected her in a way she could not understand and suddenly she wanted to be safe at home, even though this would be the first night on her own since Robbie was born. She was not as carefree as the other students thronging the bar and this questioning mature man was placing her out of her depth.

"That's the problem, Miss Brooks. We cannot know our own repressions until confronted with them in some form." He had hoped she would stay but Alice excused herself, saying she needed to get home, and so moved towards the door. "Perhaps we can discuss this some other time? Are you free for a coffee this week Miss Brooks?"

And so it was that Alice and Henry met soon after at Caruso's coffee house and she was able to talk about her interest in his selection of fabrics, and he became enchanted with the young woman's guile-less charm.

A new pattern was established. Robbie slept over at his grandparents' home on Monday nights leaving Alice free to attend lectures or meet with friends to go for a coffee, or to the cinema. She enjoyed meeting fellow students after the lectures to participate in the lively discussions. Henry Wildgoose seemed always to discover where she was and was charming and generally unruffled by the young people's often outrageous remarks. He was quick though to see flaws in their arguments but also to recognize perspicacity. Alice looked forward to these occasions as she missed the company of her peers and sometimes found herself wondering what her life might have been like if Robbie hadn't come along. She was much admired by several young men, as much for her looks and vivacity as for her thoughtful comments. She was a little different from the other young women. She was vociferous in her defence of the artist's right to challenge the way people thought and lived, even to the point of discomfort, and she fervently believed that the artist too must live a life outside the mainstream in order to nurture the creative process, and without doubt, for it was questioned by some, believed photography itself to be a great art form.

So Mr. Wildgoose became enamoured by this freethinking young woman and fascinated by the natural elegance of her body, of which she herself, he recognized, knew nothing. It was this unawareness of her own power, alongside her insightful mind, which attracted him. Again he invited her to meet him, for an evening meal he suggested, and was put out when she politely declined, giving no reason, for somehow Alice was reluctant to tell him about Robbie, perhaps fearing he would lose interest in her, as other young men had done.

***

One Saturday in February, winter loosened it's tight grip on the city, the sun came out, the cutting wind dropped and everywhere there were clumps of bright snowdrops. Alice took Robbie to Prince's Street gardens in the centre where they strolled in the

75

unexpected warmth, watching all the people thronging around, the clamour of traffic, buses, and shoppers eating in the cafes. In one of these the photographer was sitting observing the passing faces. He saw her unmistakable hair first across the road and then took in the whole scene. She was holding the hand of a small child who was wearing an unusual blue hat with a large green tassel. Quickly he paid his bill and crossed the road to intercept them.

"Hello Alice. Isn't this an amazing day?" Pointedly he didn't ask who Robbie was. Alice was startled and a little embarrassed. Her secret was out.

"Yes. Robbie and I couldn't resist coming into town. We're going to have a treat today, aren't we Robbie?

"Yes", came the eager voice of the little boy. "We're going to McDonalds and I'm going to have a banana milkshake."

His enthusiasm was infectious and Henry laughed. "They're my favourite too," he said, and then, watching for Alice's reaction,

"I've not had one for ages."

"Should you like to join us then?" she had picked up the cue and turning to her son said, "This is Mr. Wildgoose, Robbie. He is a photographer. Shall he come with us to McDonalds?"

The boy thought for a moment.

"My grandad has a camera. Alright then. You can have a banana milkshake too!"And all three of them laughed.

So it was that Henry learned about Alice's situation and for a reason he couldn't understand, this new knowledge about her life attracted him even more. Despite the fact that he'd spent the last year or more photographing children, he'd never been interested in any of them and rather disliked the way in which some mothers promoted their own needs through them, wanting fame or publicity for their offspring when really it was attention for themselves they had sought.

Why was he drawn to her, he ruminated when alone? And one answer was again underpinning his knowledge of her own unawareness of herself, of her sensuous nature, which perhaps was linked in his head to her being a mother, a fully sexual woman.

He arranged to meet her again the following Saturday with Robbie. His treat this time he had said, and decided to take them to the Museum of Contemporary Art, and for lunch. It was a blustery day. They met near the railway station and caught the circular museum bus which took them to the gallery. All the while Robbie chatted amicably with them both, he was a good natured, even-tempered child. At the gallery Henry pointed out small details in pictures and sculptures that might engage and amuse him. Alice spoke kindly and affectionately with her son with no hint of condescension and without that patronizing tone of voice which many adults seemed to use with children at that time. She gave sensible explanations at his level of understanding and often with a touch of humour. His face glowed when they shared a joke. The love between them was obvious.

She was wearing her favourite jacket again, this time with jeans and a thick cream jumper for the air was sharp. Robbie never took off his blue cap and the red-gold curls spilt around his face. Henry, who never went far without his camera, asked Alice if he might take a photo of them outside the gallery where they stood, side by side, holding hands and gazing straight out in a formal pose, quite together, marking out his separation from them.

***

By the middle of March, the course of lectures by Henry Wildgoose had finished but his guest lodgings at the University would be available for longer. The exhibition in the city also ended. He was once again a free agent. There was, however, work to do compiling and editing a book of Modern British Photography commissioned by Blackheath and Coopers publishers which specialized in contemporary art, and he could return to his base, a very small apartment and his dark room in Oxford. But Henry had a mind to extend his stay in Scotland. An old friend of his in London had offered him his recently acquired pine lodge in the Lammermuir hills so he hired a car and planned a visit. On impulse he asked Alice if she would accompany him.

"I'll have to bring Robbie," she said. "My mother deserves a break at the weekend."

"Fine, Alice. I'll pick you up, shall I?" and Alice gave him directions to her home.

Henry arrived early on the Saturday as arranged. Alice and Robbie were still finishing breakfast so invited him in. Mrs. Jenner on the landing across from Alice noticed the early morning visitor and that he was much older than her young neighbour whose situation she did not approve of. Why she must have been barely out of childhood when she'd had the bairn. What did that say about her? And now going with an older man...

"Hi Henry," Robbie was cheerful as ever. "Do you like cornflakes? We're having cornflakes and toast."

Alice's small apartment, an all in one bedsit with a box room for Robbie and a bathroom without windows, was bright and colourful unlike the uniformly dismal colours of most rented properties. Alice had spread a purple and orange throw over the sofa bed and placed a blue cloth on the table. Large posters hung on the high-ceilinged walls and one of these attracted Henry's attention immediately, for he knew the work. It was a black and white photo of a female nude leaning over a primitive washstand in a sun-flooded Provencal bathroom. It was by a French photographer Willy Ronis and Henry was an admirer of his. The subject was completely natural, not in any way a pin-up image but a delightful study of a young woman caught unawares as she was about to sponge her body with the water in the basin. The texture of the ancient wooden shutters, old stone flags and the softness of the woman's skin were skillfully photographed. The appearance was of a natural spontaneity yet Henry knew it was one of at least three dozen shots before the artist had been satisfied with the result.

"Why Alice, you have excellent taste in art!" and his compliment made her blush. Once again Henry had been caught by surprise at the unknown life of this young student.

The journey went well, Robbie and Alice sang snatches of song until Robbie became drowsy. For a while there was quiet between them, a comfortable silence. The landscape passed smoothly by, a wonderful contrast of rolling hills and small woodland copses compared with the urban geography of Edinburgh. The traffic had thinned out and then disappeared altogether as they left the main road and found a track leading to the lodge.

What was she thinking at this time? What precisely was her interest in this mature man, almost old enough to be her father? At her age wasn't it more natural to have been drawn to the young men of her own generation? Alice had few real friends. A couple of girls from her school days kept in touch and a few of the young women on her course would greet her cheerfully in the coffee bars. She had become a focus of attraction of several of the undergraduate men, but her situation with Robbie scared them off. And, of course, she was not free to come and go as them. Everything must be planned and arranged around him and she was reluctant to ask her parents to child-mind more than they were already doing. Her love for Robbie came first and satisfied her mostly. But then, this man. He was different. She admired him and he made her feel special, more significant. She was flattered by his attention and approbation. The men of her own age were only interested in her for sex-they didn't want to know about her thoughts. And he was so natural with Robbie to the extent that she wondered if he'd ever had a child himself, and suddenly his past became a mystery.

The car pulled up outside a small log cabin at the edge of woods. There was a wide clearing at the front, a log store down the side and behind, the forest trees up so close that the rooms at the back were dark.

Henry produced a key and the three of them went

in. There was a strong scent of newish pine. A small hallway led into a handsome, high ceilinged room with beams overhead and an almost full-length window at one end, which allowed the south-westerly light to illuminate the room. Floors, walls and ceiling were of pine, still new enough to be honey coloured. The back windows and a side one overlooked birch trees. There was a log burning stove, a blue sofa, two chairs, shelving for books and a desk set underneath a window, which faced south-east. A blue and white striped rug lay on the floor. On the other side of the hallway was a bathroom and a reasonably sized bedroom with its window facing out into the woodland. It had a curtained partition and a pole for hanging clothes, an enormous chest of drawers and a double bed.

It was all rather simple and rustic but the light in the main room was good and the higher than normal ceilings made the place feel spacious, even though it was in fact quite small.

"It's lovely," exclaimed Alice. Robbie was already exploring on his own. "Shall you be able to work here?"

"Well, yes, ideal really with no distractions. There's a telephone for emergencies. I'll get a lot done, the publishers want the text by the summer." Robbie was standing at the large window watching a small greenish bird fluttering from branch to branch.

"What's that mummy?" he asked but it was Henry who came over to him.

"It's a greenfinch, Robbie."

"Do you know everything about birds, Henry?" Henry laughed.

"Not everything, but I started my photographic interest by taking pictures of birds when I was boy in Derbyshire."

"Where's Derbyshire?"

"It's in England in the middle and up a bit."

"What's it like?"

"Very nice, Robbie. There are hills and dales and small villages. I was born in a town called Bakewell. They make a delicious pudding there."

And so the two chatted away whilst Alice wandered about examining the crockery and pans and exclaiming at the doll's house charm of it all.

"I'm hungry, mum," Robbie said. Henry went out to the car and returned with a large box containing their picnic lunch. He produced sausage rolls, mini meat pies, hard boiled eggs, tomatoes and apples and also a cake with blue icing which received Robbie's approval. A flask of coffee and some fruit juices were also packed in the box. The weather was still cold so the three of them sat around the kitchen table munching the food, and for the first time Henry noticed that Alice did not touch any of the meat.

"Are you vegetarian Alice?"

"Yes, I gave up eating meat when I was pregnant as suddenly I couldn't stomach it. Pregnancy can do things like that, but Robbie likes meat though."

"Birds like worms, Henry. That's meat, isn't it? They like seeds and nuts too. I feed them in my grandma's garden with bits of bacon rind she cuts up. She has a red bird visit called a robin. Grandma says I'm like a robin with my name and red hair. Robbie the robin she calls me sometimes." Alice used the moment to ask if Henry has any children and he says he thinks not, an answer to make her ponder.

After lunch they all went out to explore around the cottage and then climbed back in the car to drive back to Edinburgh.

"When shall you move in?" Alice asked, realizing with some dismay that when this happened she wouldn't see much of him.

"Soon I think. By Easter. Then I've to go down to Oxford to my flat and make some arrangements, see some people. I'll begin the book when I get back after the holidays." And Alice turned her face away from him to gaze at the view, only she didn't notice much as her thoughts of not seeing him made her sad.

***

"How are things, mum? Are you feeling better?" Grandma Sarah had a nasty cold so Alice had been shopping for her.

"I'm over the worst, I think. Robbie has been so good, haven't you dear?" She spoke fondly to her grandson. "He's helped me butter rolls, peel mushrooms and lay the table, and we've had some nice chats." There was a pause.

"He's been telling me about your exciting visit to a house in the woods, and a car journey with a man called Henry, who knows all about birds. Who is that Alice, a new friend?"

Sarah could not help herself. The thought of a strange man driving her grandson about the countryside worried her, and she wasn't sure she liked Robbie's affections being engaged elsewhere.

"He's Henry Wildgoose mum. You know the photographer who gave lectures at the University. He invited us to visit a place he's going to rent for a while so that he can write a book."

"Have you been meeting then? Isn't he much older than you?"

Sarah had noticed a tensioning of her daughter's face and guessed she wasn't being told all of it. But then what more was there? He was just a nice man Alice told herself, away from home, who liked her friendship. And Robbie's too. But she knew her parents disapproved of the recent exhibition and she didn't want to examine her own feelings too closely.

"Is this alright, Alice? He's taken all those dubious photos of children. He doesn't see Robbie on his own, does he?"And Alice exploded,

"I told you! He's an artist; he explores ideas, which some people find uncomfortable. That's his job, and I'm old enough to judge for myself about people. He's just a nice, friendly person."

But Sarah remembered what happened when Alice was sixteen and all the trauma of it.

"Well, just you be careful," and she turned to put the milk in the fridge. Lunch was eaten in a subdued atmosphere.

A week later Alice and Robbie had just arrived home and heard the telephone ringing as they opened the door, so Alice hurried to answer it. She didn't receive many calls and as she had just left her mother wondered who this was. Henry's voice was deeper on the phone and had a more noticeable Derbyshire twang than when speaking face to face.

"Hello Alice. How are you and Robbie?"

He was polite, correct. Her heart bumped and she gripped the receiver.

"We're both well, thank you. And you? Are you in

Edinburgh?"

"No. I'm at the lodge. I've just finished moving my stuff. Next week I'm off to Oxford to see my publisher and to bring back more things, books and music for my stay here. I shall remain there until after the Easter break."

Alice didn't know what to say. Was he trying to say goodbye? And then she realized how much his friendship was starting to mean.

"Alice. I've been thinking. Is it possible for you to come and see me here, on your own maybe? I'd like to take some photographs of you in the trees, Robbie would be bored I think..."

Alice's heart thumped. He wanted to see her on her own! But what about Robbie?

"I can only come on Mondays, Henry. Robbie stays with mum after preschool in the morning and overnight so it's my best day. Would that suit you?"

"I'm sure that would be OK. We'll take pot luck with the weather. I could collect you in my hired car and take you back too." So it was arranged but Alice decided not to say anything about it to her mother, or even to Robbie in case he spoke about it. She would have to hope that nothing happened whilst she was away. For the first time an element of deceit came between her and her family and Alice was uncomfortable.

***

They retraced their steps through the softening light to the cottage. Alice's body glowed and she loved the feel of his strong warm hand in hers. This lovemaking, a real and full lovemaking unlike her teenage experience, had opened her up in some mysterious way and she felt transfigured.

She looked at his face. The skin was almost harled, an outdoor skin of roughness, never quite clean-shaven and with a trace of stubble. She remembered the texture of this against her skin, and trembled a little. His lips were full and when closed as they were now gave him an aristocratic look she thought, the look of a man who lived by his own rules. She recalled this mouth recently brushing across her body all the way down from her neck, down to the hollows in her collar bone, along the curve of breasts to find a nipple and gently chew this between his teeth, then to sweep down and down over her belly towards her crotch, all this time the opening between her legs becoming soft and moist, melted and opening of its own volition. He had used his tongue to find her clitoris and tiny nibbles to arouse her more. His penetration shocked her, he fully clothed with only his member exposed, but she relished the feel of him, dominating and powerful and she dissolved into her own femaleness, into a wonderful awareness of herself.

She dared not speak as they walked along, dared not break the connection of physical intimacy. What had he felt, she wondered, but could not ask. He dropped her hand to find the key to the cabin and the spell broke.

Inside, he asked if she would like a glass of wine and as he poured this for her said;

"You will stay, won't you? I've some food planned for supper and could take you back by car early after breakfast? Or shall I drive you back now?"

And she did so want to stay. He chose some music

and carefully put it into the music player, and the sound of a piano filled the room. She sipped the rich fruity wine and curled up on the sofa watching him chop vegetables and prepare lasagna. He hummed to the music- Chopin, he said when she asked and then after a while came and sat by the fire.

"It'll be about half an hour or so. Would you like a bath?" Alice lay in the hot water, glass of wine in hand, listening to the music which echoed around the pine walls. She felt so safe, so different, so much more of herself than she had ever done in her life, even after having Robbie. He came in and sat by the bath with his own glass of wine and smiled at her. Gently he sponged soapy water over her back.

"Is this alright?" he asked and knew the answer.

The light was fading fast and it was as if the trees crept nearer the lodge, embracing it as a protection against the night. He lit candles and they ate supper and drank more wine. He talked about the book he was going to write and she listened to his views about various photographers and his ambitions. He wanted to work abroad more, he said, in the Far East or South America. She listened, transported into his imagination and her own steady, pre-ordained life seemed mundane.

They went to bed early and made love again and under cover of darkness Alice was emboldened enough to explore his nakedness, her first experience of it. She rubbed her face across his stomach and breathed deeply his male scent. She stroked his hairy soft abdomen and tentatively took his cock into her mouth, and tasted his flesh. This time, it was he who gasped, when the orgasm came, and afterwards they fell asleep together, warm between the duvets until light seeped in the next morning.

The drive back to Edinburgh was over far too quickly. Alice was now unsure about what would happen next.

"When are you going to Oxford?" she asked.

"Tomorrow. I'll be gone for three weeks. Shall I see you when I get back?" and the fact that he had asked the question both pleased and dismayed her. Rather, much rather, she would have preferred him to say more, to have said he was sorry to be away for so long, that he would contact her from Oxford; that he would be thinking of her all the time.

"Yes," she replied, "give me a ring," as coolly as she could, and he dropped her outside her flat and drove away.

***

Alice could not easily pick up her usual routine in the weeks that followed but her mother's exhortation to be careful came into her mind. She was sure that Henry must have some feelings for her after what had happened. If he'd wanted to dump her he'd surely not have said he'd get in touch again. Despite her experience of conceiving Robbie the thought of contraception hadn't occurred to her but if they were going to have sex again her mother's words took on another meaning and so she visited her G.P. and was prescribed the Pill, just in case.

That Easter was a difficult time for Alice. Her parents flew to Malta for a holiday leaving her totally alone with her little boy. Normally this would have been a pleasure but with Henry away too and her feelings and thoughts in a turmoil, she was restless and unfocused. She tried to get on with her studies whenever the opportunity arose but found herself daydreaming. One project, however, was influenced by the lovemaking in Spring Wood. She was to design a seasonally inspired furnishing fabric- the first actual design project of the course and Alice used a recurring image of graceful, wild daffodils, creamy and lemon, against a pale fawn background and tiny greenfinches dotted about. She was very pleased with the result.

The days passed and nobody rang, and no post of any significance arrived. She began to feel miserable. Why hadn't he given her his address in Oxford or a telephone number? So that she couldn't get in touch? But then, on the Thursday after Easter she received several items all at once: a postcard for Robbie (of a greenfinch), an amusing letter for her and a postcard for them both from Malta.

Robbie loved the picture of the bird he had seen in the wood and wanted to paint his own version so Alice traced a bold outline on a sheet of paper and he mixed his own paints.

"I could do a robin next time, mum, for grandma, for when she gets back." So Alice and he went into town to the library to find a child's Illustrated Book of British Birds, and bought some more crayons and paints. Alice was good at drawing so could quickly make simple outlines for Robbie to colour in. Together they made a colour chart so that he might learn which colours when mixed together made the shades he needed and for a child so young he was quick to learn. Now he wanted to go out to parks and gardens so that he could look for different birds.

Henry had written affectionately and with humour describing the events of his time in Oxford. He didn't mention the lovemaking in the wood, or her visit to the lodge, only to say he was looking forward to seeing her again but this was enough. Her spirits lifted. Suddenly life seemed full of possibilities once more.

The summer term began and still she didn't know if Henry had returned and could only wait, each day hoping for a phone call or another letter. Robbie was now making pictures of birds for Henry, sure in the way that children can be that he would be seeing him again.

One early evening, after she and Robbie were about to prepare supper together, for the boy was a willing helper and liked chopping vegetables and could do it with unexpected care, the buzzer on the front door rang and opening it she was surprised to see Henry standing there.

"I hope this is alright, Alice. I was in Edinburgh to see someone at the University and thought I'd drop by. I should have phoned, I know."

He grinned in the disarming way he had and, of course, she asked him in.

"Hi Robbie, how are you? Did you have any Easter eggs?"

"Henry!! Yes, I had two eggs, one from mummy and another from my grandma and grandad, that one had icing flowers with my name on it and mum's had chocolate buttons inside it!" He was excited, very pleased to see Henry again and openly fond. Henry produced a package from a bag and gave it to him. The boy eagerly tore at the brown paper and pulled out a hand bound book of photos of garden birds.

These are some of the photos I took myself Robbie when I was about fourteen. I thought you might like to have some."

Robbie and Alice were thrilled, and the little boy rushed off to his bedroom to find his painting for Henry.

"That's very thoughtful of you." Alice smiled, "He's been getting very interested in birds. He'll love you for it."

"And here's something for you Alice. I hope it will be helpful in your studies." Her gift was a beautifully illustrated book about the weaving designs of the Navajo Indians in New Mexico.

Such carefully chosen presents convinced Alice that Henry must genuinely like them both. She cooked supper for all three of them, a cheese and tomato pizza, Robbie's favourite, and as she put him to bed Henry sat and looked at her coursework files and the pattern design for the spring fabric.

"This is nice, Alice, I like it," as she came back into the room and she blushed, partly for the praise, partly for the remembrance.

"There were daffodils in the woods where you took the photos," she said, looking at him for a reaction.

He smiled. "Yes, indeed, I remember it well." They sat together on the sofa bed as the evening light faded.

"Are you going back tonight?"

"Well, I've nowhere else to sleep, unless..."

Now this produced a conflict of feelings in her; of course she wanted to be with him in bed again, but

Robbie was just a few yards away and she wasn't sure about that, if the time was right, but was she being immature about this? What should she do?

"Are you worried about what Robbie might think?" He was sensitive to her hesitation.

"Well yes. What if he walks in? He's never seen me in bed with a man."

"He'll have seen his grandparents in bed. Won't it seem normal?"

So Henry stayed and made love to her considerately, quietly, gently, and so they slept together until the early morning light woke them. Henry was dressed and out of the flat before Robbie got up but Mrs. Jenner, an early riser, was standing at her sitting room window watching the street below, drinking her mug of tea and saw the man leave the building and shook her head at such goings-on, and her with a little bairn too.

The weeks that followed through April and May brought fine weather and a roller coaster of emotions for Alice. When she wasn't with Henry her mind couldn't focus on her life without him and when she was with him her feelings swung from elation to a churning anxiety. She wanted so much to please him and found it easy to acquiesce to his sexual desires which increasingly seemed to be driven by a need to experiment, to keep his anticipation stimulated. For the first time she began to see herself as a sexual creature, not just a mother, and she scoured second hand shops and sales for different clothes. She acquired some red stiletto heeled shoes, a suspender belt and white lace stockings and flaunted her legs at him. Another time she wore a black basque after her evening bath and paraded around the room, her waist pulled in tightly (she needed him to fasten it at the back) so that her breasts were pushed upwards almost exposing the nipples, and the cut-away back revealed the pale sloping globes of her buttocks. She bought red lipstick and a thin black velvet choker. He loved the transition from wholesome young student to experienced provocative woman after she had arrived at the lodge and took photos of her from all angles. Her body seemed always to be in a semi-aroused state and he caught scent of this, and his need for sex with her grew. He made love to her against the birches outside, or in the rain, in the sitting room and in the bath, during the day and outside in the dark amongst the woodland creatures, using many positions. And all the while she was both submissive and supreme.

Every Monday now she caught the train to Dunbar and he collected her by car and returned her early on Tuesday mornings. Her parents and Robbie knew nothing of this and her mind was always troubled by this dual life. What if Robbie had an accident or fell ill and needed her when she was away? Her relationship with Henry was changing, and she was deeply caught up with his identity. She admired everything about him.

He had arranged things at the lodge to suit himself. He'd brought in many books, of photography, poetry, novels and writings about philosophy. There was a striking picture of an Indian city and several images of a very beautiful Asian girl dressed in a gorgeous sari. She asked about this, was she someone he knew and his brief answer of 'Yes' somehow prevented her from asking any further questions. He had a classical music collection, and would play at full volume the voices of Janet Baker and Jessye Norman and compositions of Schubert, Wagner and Beethoven. He would open the windows wide and the music filtered through the trees. But she was ignorant of much of his life. He spoke little of his growing up in Derbyshire his father had been editor of a county magazine and his mother had died when he was fifteen, he didn't say how. Alice was always reluctant to probe sensing that he didn't like this, therefore much of his past remained unknown to her. She gathered information in tiny amounts and tried to make links. There was a smallish framed photograph on the bookshelf of a young woman with blonde hair and an inscription at the bottom which read:-

To my special friend

Was it from her, or to her? Who was she? Alice was afraid to ask. Why did he have it still? Was the woman seeing him? Was she in Oxford?

Once, back in Edinburgh, as she was walking between her flat and the university, she saw him further down across the street, or thought she saw him by the time she crossed the traffic he had disappeared. She asked him the next Monday if he'd been in Edinburgh that day and he said he didn't think so. The answer seemed evasive. Anxiety now fed her growing obsession for him and just when she was convinced he didn't really care for her and was using her he gave her a small but carefully chosen gift, something that changed her mind. She'd be happy again. He did love her really, it was just circumstances that kept them apart. He needed the space for his work and she had Robbie to look after and not much room at her flat. When he did come to her there she was always on edge. He was ever kind to Robbie and appeared truly fond of him but she didn't want her child to talk about him to her parents.

Her father would ask her how things were going, was she enjoying the course, working well, had she made some friends ... and her mother remained silent, pursing her lips as Alice replied, making no mention of Henry.

At weekends the whole world seemed to be composed of couples strolling hand-in-hand in the early summer sun and Alice wondered what he did then and tried to telephone him at different times. Often her calls went unanswered and she became convinced that he was seeing someone else and looked for signs of this when she was there. Frequently, however, he seemed to disappear.

On June 4 Robbie was four years old and a party for his friends from play school and pre-school groups was organized by Sarah and Alice. Nine children came to her parent's house as it had more space. They played games in the garden and ate tea as a picnic. The other mothers were in their late twenties and Alice felt as if she didn't quite fit. There had still been no news from Henry who had been silent for over a week.

Then one Saturday at breakfast he telephoned to say that he was in Edinburgh and could he take her and Robbie out for the day. Fortuitously she had no other plans and so quickly she and Robbie got dressed and met him in town. He'd travelled in by train. They walked as a threesome in the sunshine for all the world as if they were a family. He had his camera and stopped to take photos every now and then if there were scenes of interest to him, with Robbie now skipping along in front of them. A blue planter full of orange marigolds, a laconic youth clad in black leathers sitting on his motorbike and lighting a cigarette. Once he was asked by a passer-by if they would like a group picture taking and Henry handed over his camera, explaining which button to press, and the three of them stood close together, relaxed and happy.

Henry took them to a cafe for lunch and then produced three tickets for an outdoor theatrical event for children, about a boy who'd befriended a lion. It was he said, a belated birthday present. The little boy was excited beyond measure and as they climbed into the wooden seats, his eyes shone.

"This is my favourite bit!" he exclaimed and Alice and Henry both laughed.

"But you've not seen the show yet!" Both recognized that the anticipation was as thrilling as the event itself for the child.

Afterwards they returned to her flat and Henry stayed, and this time Alice didn't mind that her son knew. Unexpectedly, on the following Sunday morning, a car pulled up outside the apartment and Robbie saw, with enthusiasm, his grandparents getting out.

"Hi grandma and grandad!" he yelled with delight and rushed to the door. Alice was horror-struck. Fortunately the bedding had been stowed away and the sofa bed put back to normal but she knew it was too early in the day for her to be having a male friend. Henry, however, was unperturbed.

"Hello, darling!" her mother swooped Robbie up for a hug as she came in and her husband followed from behind. Both stopped when they saw their daughter's visitor but Henry went forward, easily and in full control, and introduced himself.

"Hello, I'm Henry Wildgoose, a friend of Alice and Robbie, how do you do?" Alice's face had flushed as deeply as her hair, and both parents then understood that the word 'friend' was a euphemism.

Robbie was overflowing with news of the play they had seen and his grandparents replied saying that as it was such a lovely day they'd thought of driving to the seaside, to North Berwick. Would Henry like to join them?

James had realized immediately when Henry introduced himself who the photographer was and had quickly decided that he should use the opportunity to get to know something about this controversial man, for he had sensed the emotional engagement towards him from his daughter's reactions. He would try to elicit the character of the man for himself.

The weather was glorious and North Berwick was busy with visitors. When Robbie spotted a poster showing an image of a gannet with its amazing ice-cool eyes he asked what it was. Henry replied.

"It's a solan goose, also known as a gannet. You see that huge rock out at sea, Robbie? That's called Bass Rock and it's an ancient volcanic plug and home to one of the largest breeding colonies of the solan goose in the world!"

The bird was the emblem for the Scottish Sea Bird Centre, explained Henry, and the boy tugged at his grandma's hand.

"Please can we go in, grandma? To see the birds!"

James liked the manner the photographer used with his grandson. He obviously respected the child, and didn't patronize him. He seemed to want to expand his knowledge, so they all went into the Centre, much to Robbie's delight.

James enjoyed Henry's company. He quickly realized that here was an intelligent, thoughtful man, very much his own person, an equal with him and his wife, a man who knew his own worth. He felt he had a genuine affection for his daughter, and wondered if this friendship would be a steadying influence upon her. In return Henry liked James for he was an urbane, civilized person, thoroughly decent and honest.

Sarah, however, was more cautious. For her, the age difference between Alice and Henry was too great, and besides, Alice had at least two more years of study ahead of her, and he, she intuitively understood, was not a man to settle in one place to a domestic life. In fact, she wondered why, or if, he was not already married.

***

At the end of June, Henry told Alice he was going back to Oxford for a while, to meet his publisher and make some arrangements. She was sitting on his sofa with the light streaming in setting her red-gold hair aflame with colour. He combed his fingers through it and drew her to him, and for once her compliance annoyed him. Her disappointment was obvious and he felt slightly irritated. Her emotional dependency on him was unsettling for he knew she had made few friends. He felt restless after the long slog of writing and editing; felt in need of change, a new project and he was looking forward to revisiting Oxford and London again to catch up with the art scene.

Alice wondered if she could visit him whilst he was away, perhaps her parents would have Robbie for a few days. She could come down by train and began to eagerly search for her diary in her bag. When she put the question, Henry quickly responded.

"No, no Alice. I don't think that's a good idea. I'll have a lot of boring meetings; the publisher, the bank manager. No, much better if I get it all done on my own as quickly as I can."

Alice could not easily disguise her misery. She struggled to keep tears away and wondered what was going to happen when his rental contract at the lodge ran out. She had tried not to think about this but his visit to Oxford brought home the reality of her uncertain future. Her University year was ending, she'd passed the exams to go on for the second year and the long summer vacation was ahead. She really needed to get some paid work as money was quite tight, and all of a sudden her happiness with Henry seemed like a mirage and reality loomed.

He was gone for a month and his calls and letters were scant. She endured his absence with great difficulty. Her moods became erratic and she was often cross with Robbie over the slightest thing. She had taken a part-time job serving in a cafe and hated every minute of it.

Then at the end of July he telephoned her from the lodge. He was back and looking forward to seeing her! Overjoyed, she telephoned the cafe saying she was unwell and caught the Monday train to Dunbar. He was wanting to see her as soon as she was back. Perhaps whilst away, he had realized how much he'd missed her?

Hardly had they got through the door of the lodge when he began to hurriedly take off her clothes and bending her over the table entered her from behind. The urgency and lust of it swept through her, awakening again those deep sensuous places of her body. Surely, now, he must know he loved her as she did him?

After lunch they walked through the trees. The summer foliage was deep green, heavy and oppressive. The light was dim and there were no flowers. She felt uncomfortable.

"I love the peace of the wood," he said, "after the noise and bustle of cities."

"Do you think you could live without a city life?" She asked the question, imagining a life with him and Robbie in a house in the hills.

He thought for a moment.

"This is lovely to come back to, but you know, Alice, I'm a photographer. There's a limit to the pictures I could take in one place. As a matter of fact, I've been talking to some people at the National Geographic about a foreign project."

Alice became very still inside, shocked into a kind of internal paralysis. What did this mean? Her brain had stopped processing information.

"Are you going away? Where will you be?" The questions stumbled out of her at last, despite her intuitive understanding that he wouldn't like to be interrogated, that she ought to wait for him to tell her when he wanted to.

"I don't know yet, Alice. There are a few possibilities." He was vague, unwilling to upset her for he liked her greatly, but mindful and protective of his own interests.

"Let's wait and see. I'll know in a few weeks time. Now let me cook you a lovely supper. You choose some music and have a bath and I'll get the meal going", and his tone was reassuring, loving. Alice suddenly wondered if she and Robbie could go with him. She could look after him, cook for him. She could delay her studies for a while, and so lying in the warm, soapy bath she began to plan. Robbie wasn't at school until next Easter; she could take two terms out and travel with Henry. She was used to living simply. It wouldn't cost much surely and she could investigate textile traditions as a form of research for her degree. Excitedly, she began to flesh out a life with him.

Ten days later, Henry rang her bell. Alice was alone, Robbie having gone to a friend's birthday party and her parents to Gairloch for a fortnight's holiday.

"I'm so glad to see you Henry. I've been thinking a lot and have a great idea. I want to tell you about it. Coffee or tea?" She was very excited and dashed to the sink to fill the kettle before he could answer.

"Just a minute Alice. I've got some news I must tell you first" and then something in his manner made her pause.

"Is everything alright? No problems with your book?"

He sat down on a chair as Alice remained by the sink, the kettle in her hand.

"I've heard yesterday from National Geographic. They've offered me a contract for a year in Papua New Guinea. It's a major project quite a large team are going. I'm to photograph wild life and also there is an expedition in search of indigenous natives. There are still many undiscovered tribes in the forests it's thought. It's a wonderful opportunity for me, Alice."

"No, no Henry. That's too far away! It's the other side of the world."

She was utterly dismayed. Her legs began to feel unstable and she sat down heavily on the sofa. Henry didn't move. He was going away and didn't comfort her. Why didn't he come to her and put his arms around her and tell her she must go with him? He faced her from his seat, but yards of space and a chasm of half the globe away.

"I'm to leave soon, Alice. The rains end in September and then the expedition will begin. We're all to get there quickly to acclimatize and prepare." His voice was calm, but he had known this meeting would be difficult yet the look on her face worried him. He carried on.

"I'm to fly out to Sydney first, then on to Port Moresby..."

"But Henry," Alice interrupted, her voice increasingly shrill, "we could come with you, Robbie and me. I've been thinking it through. Robbie doesn't start school until next Easter. Coming with you I'll be able to look after you while you work. It would be a great adventure for Robbie too. I'll borrow the money for our fare, we'd manage somehow, maybe dad would let me sublet the flat for..."

"Wait Alice!" He held up his hand to stop her. "It's

impossible. It's tropical jungle out there. I'll not be just in one place, they'll be others as well, and it's not a safe life for Robbie. There are malarial mosquitoes, parasites and snakes. We will be on the move a lot."

Alice, desperate now, knowing in her heart before her head, that he'd come to say goodbye, perhaps forever, began to shout.

"Please Henry, take us with you. I love you so much. Robbie loves you. I can't bear it if you go."

"Alice, truly, it's not possible."

"Take me then. If Robbie is a problem I can ask mum and dad to look after him for a while. I'll come with you. Henry, please don't leave me." And Alice screamed her pleas regardless of the noise she made.

Henry was shocked.

"You can't leave Robbie behind! He's much too young, he needs you. He needs to be here, with his family. I'm not his father. He'll forget me."

"But what about me? You love me! You need me with you!"

"I've never said that Alice. You know I've never said those things." The words stunned her. Across the landing, Mrs. Jenner, her ear pressed to the door, heard sobbing and the man's deep persistent voice.

"It's better this way. My work will always come first. We've had a good few months of friendship. I'll always remember that. You have a great future in front of you. You are a gifted and beautiful young woman and one day you'll meet the love of your life and you and your child will be cared for as you should be. I'm a wanderer. I don't know what my future holds but this is too good an opportunity for me to turn down. Perhaps, if you hadn't got Robbie, it might have been possible for a while, but you would be giving up your own ambitions and future trailing round places with me; when I'd be off photographing you'd be left in some awful hut on your own. No. It's just not possible".

He tried to make it easier for her to bear, for truly he was upset by her distress. He'd known she cared for him deeply, more deeply he now realized than he for her, but she'd seemed cool enough about his comings and goings, hadn't pressed him for information, had got on with her studies, her own life. And she and Robbie, they were the couple really.

He stood up slowly and moved towards the door and Alice ran to him, to hold him fast, her tears soaking her face and her hair wild and bushy.

"Don't go Henry. Please don't go away." But he closed the door behind him and left her the other side of it crying bitterly on the floor.

Alice spent the next week in a tumult of emotions, listing from despair to dullness, to desperate clinging to Robbie. There was nobody she could unburden herself to. Nobody but Henry would have understood. Robbie had picked up his mother's unhappiness and become fractious. Henry's words swam around her head all the time. She couldn't think clearly, couldn't sleep and would have to get up and pace the floor. In the evenings she'd drink wine to numb her feelings. In the daytime she would take Robbie out into the streets to walk endlessly, to try and tire herself out. She remembered the pale daffodils in the woods and wept.

Robbie tried to console her in his childish way. He helped at mealtimes, laying the table and taking dirty dishes to the sink. One morning he made his own bed thinking it would please her. He crept close to her on the sofa, climbed on to her lap needing her reassurance and wanting to reassure her, but she was immune to these attempts to comfort her. Her thoughts were always of Henry, his leaving and, briefly, a flicker of hope that he might change his mind, that even now he would be remembering their lovemaking and would realize his feelings for her and pick up the telephone.

She tried to phone him but it just rang and rang. After three days she suddenly decided to go and see him at the Lodge and took Robbie to the station for the train to Dunbar. She tried to catch a bus but none went near the wood so she hired a taxi and spent far too much money. Before she got out of the cab she could see that the place was shut up but she banged on the door all the same. Nothing. Emptiness. The taxi driver had waited with Robbie. He could see what was up and reduced his fare out of kindness. It was a miserable journey back to Edinburgh.

That night, Alice had a nightmare. She was in bed with Henry and they had made love, but then he turned to her and he was wearing a dark hood with eye-slits. He pointed to the door and she knew she must go to it, go to her own execution in the woods. Henry had a large axe in his hand and slowly she went to the door, knowing it must be so, her fear making her clumsy, her nakedness making her shiver. At the door, near the edge of the wood, the path was lined with giant daffodils leading to a block. Henry wrapped a scarlet blanket around her and stroked her hair one last time. She woke up trembling, and sweating with fear.

A week to the day he had told her his plans, Alice switched on the television after supper. Robbie was in the bath next door and she wandered between the rooms. There was an early evening programme showing about culture and the arts but she wasn't really listening. Robbie was sitting in the bath playing with his toy boat.

Suddenly, a familiar voice spoke out of the TV and Alice turned to look, her heart thudding furiously as Henry's face appeared in front of her, larger than life.

"Yes, it's a marvellous opportunity for me." He was being interviewed.

"You know the birds in Papua New Guinea are so exotic, and there are the monkeys, of course. There will be a team of us Michael Woodlake's work you know already and Katherine Alsop's, I particularly enjoyed her recent exhibition here in Oxford. I'm looking forward to collaborating with them both. It's a major investment by the National Geographic. We'll have a botanist and an anthropologist amongst others. I'm flying out from Heathrow tomorrow."

His voice faded as the interviewer gave thanks. "That was Henry Wildgoose speaking from the studio in Oxford, recorded two days ago. We look forward in the future to seeing the results of his expedition."

Two days ago! Flying out tomorrow! He had already gone! All her hopes and dreams were wiped out as on a magic slate. She heard a noise, like a cow in labour, and looked around startled but a part of her brain registered that the sound had come from her own body, a bellow of pain. She heard noises in her head and there was a pain deep in her chest and screams poured from her throat. She raged and sobbed and seeing a half full bottle of whisky Henry had left behind began to swig huge gulps to deaden her despair.

Stumbling, she fell against the sofa, unseeing, unaware of her screams of loss and anguish. She didn't hear the cries of Robbie, distressed at his mother's behaviour, frightened; she didn't hear him call out to her, "mummy, mummy, what's happening?" She didn't hear the ominous slide as his feet slipped on a bar of soap as he endeavoured to climb out of the bath to go to her; didn't hear the crack of his skull as it hit the metal tap; didn't hear the splash of water as he fell, face down into the bath.

But eventually she did hear the unnatural silence. When she gained some control of herself and came a little to her senses, an empty quietness pervaded the flat.

"Robbie! Robbie!" and she ran into the bathroom. The little boy was gently bobbing in the water. His golden hair floated on the surface like maidenhair fern in a pool. And his arms gently swayed by his sides. The bath water was still, the little toy boat hardly moving.

Knowledge comes to us before thought sometimes. Alice knew immediately that he was dead, knew this before she lifted his soft pliant body into her arms, the water streaming off him and over her. She knew this before she saw his lifeless eyes, the inner light switched off. She knew he was dead and that it was completely her fault.

Cradling him to her she keened and rocked him in her arms as if she were rocking him to sleep. She wrapped him up in a towel to keep him warm and lay on the sofa with him, murmuring to him;

"Don't leave me Robbie, don't go, I love you so much. Please don't go."

Half an hour passed. Perhaps more. She was cold, wet, numb. Gently she laid his body on the sofa and made a 999 telephone call.

"It's my boy Robbie, He's dead. I killed him." The police and medics arrived together. Mrs. Jenner was waiting on the landing.

"It was awful, the shouting. She's hurt him, hasn't she? That man she had, he didn't want him, did he?" And she was still there, sometime later, when a small, covered body was taken out on a stretcher, and afterwards, when Alice Brooks was led away in handcuffs.

PART THREE

John trembles but Alice is calm, quiet now. She has spoken the harsh words, 'I killed him,' and there is an acceptance in her voice, a recognition of a truth long held. She turns to look at him, exhaustion showing in the puffed, bruised looking flesh beneath her eyes, but her concern is for him.

"This is hard for you John, to hear these things. I am sorry to cause you this pain."

He can't quite access his feelings. Is it that he'd thought there must be some mistake, a mix-up of identity, a confusion of stories? Is he angry, disappointed, afraid? She has said those words 'I killed him,' sitting on his sofa, speaking of her young child, 'I killed him.' Yet the account of Robbie's death, which has caused his eyes to become wet, suggests something else. He is confused.

Alice stands and sways a little, and John gets up too. "I'll get some food, you must eat something, then you can sleep in Claire's room."

She searches for his hand and presses it slightly. For a reason he cannot fathom, her gratitude and concern for him produces a rush of compassion, which takes him by surprise.

Toast and cheese are quietly put on the table but little is eaten. He leads her to the back bedroom, not overlooked at all, and she gets under the duvet still in her clothes and he covers her up carefully, switches off the light and gently closes the door. It is the middle of the night. His mind is still reeling with all that he has heard, yet he realizes that there is so much more to know. What has happened to her all these years? He lies down on his own bed, also fully dressed. No one can know she is here, but he must discover what is happening in the village. Even Jennie will think she is still away. Hopefully nobody will visit the car park at the back of the Ben for a while. Can he persuade her to stay with him until he knows what to do?

Early next morning he leaves her a note on the kitchen table along with breakfast foods. He'll be back at lunchtime and wishes her to remain in his house at the very least till then.

He opens up his office and tries to deal with correspondence. The advert for staff is to go out that day. At 11 o'clock he drives into the village and goes to the shop for a few items but really because he wants to pick up any gossip. His sister is behind the counter.

"Have you heard the awful news, John? Folk are really angry that she's come to live here. There's a lot of talk of escorting the bairns to school and back."

"Do they really think she's come to kill all our children?" He snarls, contemptuous of the easy way some people will adopt hysteria, but knowing too, his own unexpressed fears, for what crime is possibly worse than a mother killing her own child?

"John! She's a self-confessed murderer! How do we know she won't kill again? I've told Alistair and David to keep together. Some of the younger bairns have already heard things and are frightened. I even heard talk of a vigilante group. Aye Malcolm McKenzie and his boys are whipping things up but I hear the Minister went to see him and has put a stop to it." And it occurs to John that maybe he ought to speak to Revd. McMillan himself. But first he will return home and see how Alice is. He needs to know a great deal more before he considers what is best.

Alice is still asleep when he returns to his house. He re-writes the note saying it isn't safe for her to go home yet that she can stay here for a while, and to keep the curtains drawn and not to answer the door or use the telephone.

Back in his office, the adverts are sent off and John sits and thinks. On a whim he telephones Esther Patterson and is comforted to hear her bright voice. He is learning to respect and admire this lady and needs an ally.

"Mrs. Patterson? Good afternoon. It's John Stewart at the Centre. I wonder if I might have a few minutes of your time?"

"Please do call me Esther and I shall call you John, shall I? It's so much more comfortable, don't you think?"

"Well, I'm pleased to, Esther. But I'm really ringing you about a rather serious matter, about this news of Alice Brooks." He is cautious, feels protective.

"Yes, I thought it might be that. It's so sad, isn't it? That poor woman."

Just like the kind heart she is to show compassion, John thinks, not to condemn until she understands more. It might be possible to confide in her.

"Do you know anything more than the rumours, Esther?" He is aware that she has met Alice privately. There is a pause.

"Well, actually John, I've been making some

private enquiries myself. My late husband had medical contacts at Cornton Vale prison. I'm afraid it is true that Miss Brooks was imprisoned there for fifteen years before her parole."

John holds his breath. His chest feels tight. He doesn't know what to say.

"Are you still there, John? Perhaps we could meet for a chat? I've other information but I rather not speak over the phone." So John arranges to visit Esther later the following morning. He returns home again at half past four and is glad to see that from the outside there is no sign of Alice. The bungalow is quiet when he enters and for a moment he fears that she has left, but there she is curled up on the sofa, staring into space.

"John, are you alright? This is very difficult for you, but you've been so kind to me. Perhaps you think I have betrayed your trust?" Her voice is quiet, dignified, but she speaks with genuine concern he feels, and is touched.

"Alice I can't begin to tell you what a terrible shock it is for all of us. There is some hysteria in the village. I'm afraid it really isn't safe for you to go home just now. I'd like to hear the rest of your story. I feel sure you didn't kill Robbie, I just can't comprehend it. It's obvious that you loved him, and you've described a hideous accident. Why, in that case, were you sent to Cornton Vale?"

And so Alice reluctantly agrees to stay. He cooks some supper and keeps the curtain closed against the world, and afterwards they sit together before the burning logs.

John stares into the flames. He remains confused,

scared. What is he feeling? It is as if the ground beneath him has been shaken, for previously he had thought perhaps that in Alice there might be a new beginning for himself. Now this possibility has vanished. How can he re-invent himself when his trust in her has been wiped away?

Alice watches his face. Why is she here in his home? Surely, she can go to her own place, collect some things, drive to Fort William or Edinburgh, indeed anywhere, stay in a hotel and decide then what to do. Maybe she can walk into the village openly, unafraid for she has faced much worse than the rage of ill-informed, small minds, and surely there will be some whose innate sense of decency will not judge her too easily. Why does she feel she owes John an explanation?

Slowly, mindfully, Alice picks up the threads of her story, the weft threads which weave themselves in and out of the invisible warp, which constitute the foundation of the fabric of our being.

"John, this is difficult to hear and to say. I offered no defence at my trial. I refused to speak. My mother was distraught, and would not attend the court. My father came every day in his grey suit but looking very pale. I could not look him in the face. I refused to plead. All around me people bustled and advised, became impatient, angry. I was roughly handled. I did not care about any of it. Whilst the case continued I sank down in myself to a place of blankness, a non-place, colourless, silent, without texture. I became thin and unwashed. A woman was brought in to clean me up. I indicated that I wanted all my hair cut off hence the short spikes which became the world image that you have seen. I never wore it long since that time. My father gave testimony, citing my friendship as he put it with Henry Wildgoose.

None of this helped me at all for it was known that Henry had had criticism levelled at him for misusing children in his photographic work and I on trial for killing my child. A rudimentary search for him was made, but he was out of contact, they said. Mrs. Jenner gave evidence about what she had heard said on the stairs. She also said that she believed Robbie was in the way of my going with Henry, said that I drank a lot and was immoral. My emotions were skewered. I didn't care what happened to me for I had lost Robbie. It was my own selfish need that had caused my child's death. I could not bear the pain. I felt that I had in essence killed him so deserved punishment. And that came swift and savage. In November 1980 I was sent to Cornton Vale prison for twenty years and the doors closed against the world.

Did you know, John, that most women in prison are ill? They are mentally or emotionally disturbed, suffer addictions and ill health and have often been abused. Most ought not to be there at all for no good comes of it. But I, a rare breed, a convicted murderer from a good background was different. Fear spread through the prison when it was known I was coming. Fear and then inevitably rage, all the repressed anger which abused women do not know how to deal with other than harm themselves. Now all that would be vented upon me. I was kept apart for my own safety whilst they calmed down, but each time I had to leave my cell, always under escort, the screaming and banging would start again. If I came near enough to anyone I would be spat at and invectives spewed at me, yet these were often women who by their behaviour had forfeited the right to keep their own children who were now probably suffering themselves in care homes. I was to pay the communal price. Hatred is a kind of disguised fear, I think. The atmosphere in the jail after my arrival was thick and oppressive. The staff were jumpy and inclined to project their own frustrations on to me too. The worst kind of offence they said ... unimaginable to kill one's own child. I was a monster.

I was unaware what the newspapers and television companies were saying about me. My parents suffered terribly and my mother rarely left the house. I had ruined their lives as well as my own and all the while I was mute, anaesthetized by an abiding anguish; couldn't eat, wouldn't clean myself, just wanted oblivion. And when life did flicker in me, as it will, the pain then was worse and the awareness of it increased in potency. I needed death. My father came to visit, quiet and grey. For a time I refused to see him but he kept coming every week making the journey from Edinburgh and back without seeing me. Then I agreed to meet him but sat, catatonic he later said he was appalled at my plight and wondered how he and my mother could survive it. He pressurized the governor to provide better medical care. I was then given medication and a woman was brought in to care for my personal needs, and gradually, very gradually, I began to surface. The tumult in the prison had died down but when I was first allowed out with a warder as escort into the refectory, there was uproar. The women threw their food at me and screamed abuse, and so it continued until the rage simmered down. I was handled roughly, clawed, threatened with unspeakable violence.

As I was slowly roused from my utter despair, I felt the urgent need to inflict pain upon myself and at any opportunity would try to slice my arms.The physical pain was wonderful I craved it, it released some inner terrors.

Then came news of my mother's illness. She had discovered a lump in her left breast, and was to undergo surgery, and then chemotherapy. She still would not see me, and dad now had two women to wrench at his heart. The illness was short the disease was aggressive and spread quickly and within a year she died. That was 1984 and I had only served four years of my term. This loss re-ignited the terrible suffering I had first experienced, but this time, because my father was laid low with it all, I felt completely alone. I wanted to die, needed to die, only death would be a solution to all this misery. I wanted to be with Robbie and my mother and say to them how sorry I was, but how to do it? I wasn't under the constant surveillance I had been when I first came into prison but opportunity and method were difficult to find. So I tried what others had done. I swallowed a tampon several in fact forcing them down my throat with my fingers and then drinking water until they swelled and choked me. I failed, my body's automatic response and the sounds it made alerted a passing warder and I was resuscitated. After that I was watched and guarded day and night. I slept as best I could under naked electric lights, yet these were the darkest times of all. Occasionally a remembrance of

Henry would fill my head unasked for, unwanted, and the image of pale daffodils seemed to be engraved in the retinas of my eyes. And then the crying began. Without warning the tears just poured out and my body sobbed until I ached with it all; it was as if my body itself was trying to shake out, through water, the great sadness it had kept to itself all this time. The water that Robbie had drowned in came streaming out of me for weeks and weeks, and month after month. Gradually the crying began to reduce until, after a year or more, there were no tears left.

Dad still came, still watched over me heaven only knows what his life was like then. One day it was as if I was seeing him for the first time after a long absence. I gazed at him with new sight. He was frail now; his shoulders had once been strong and straight, but had become thin and curved, and his jacket hung on him as if it were not his own. The skin on the back of his hands had some liver spots already and was loose. And there was a sadness in his eyes which never left him, even when he smiled and spoke with his cheerful voice.

"How are things today, Alice?" he'd say. "You're looking better. I've left some books for you in reception. There's a parcel for you too, a little surprise." And later I'd be given some sweet smelling bars of soap, or maybe a tin of talcum powder. I looked at him then and realized we were both prisoners and my heart went out to him. I wanted to hug and comfort him. I wanted to tell him how sorry I was for causing so much grief."

John is close to tears himself. There is something both powerful and unreal in the story he is now processing of Alice's experiences. How is this being created? Is it her calm manner the way she sits with her head up and her eyes focused as if she sees herself somewhere else? Her voice, low but clear, with expression but under control? Or is it the way her hands held in her lap lift and fold the air from time to time? There she sits, almost serene, recounting episodes of loss, death, attempted suicide, victimization, grief, and now compassion.

John stirs. "I'm going to pour a whisky. Can I get you anything, Alice?" He speaks lovingly. What can he possibly get her? She sits on the sofa a chasm away, yet she feels the warmth and concern and so smiles, her eyes alert again, her expression alive.

"Yes, thank you John. I would like a cup of tea." He goes to fill the kettle, glad to be doing something for her, however insignificant. The wind is getting up outside and the logs are sinking to ash. It is well into the night.

"I think we should sleep now" he says, and as the words are spoken he knows he wants to lie with her and hold her close in the darkness, sharing warmth, companionship, and Alice knows too what he wants but is not ready for it herself. They sleep apart.

***

The following morning John drives to the Patterson house and is greeted at the door.

"It's so good of you to come John. Please do come in out of the weather", and she shows him into her sitting room where a tray is already laid with china cups and saucers, jug and sugar bowl. The fire is bright in the grate.

"I'll not be a minute now. You make yourself at

home. Shall you prefer coffee or tea?"

"Coffee for preference, please."And she leaves him to attend to this.

The room is spacious and light and decorated in an elegant assortment of pale pastel colours. Fine paintings hang on the walls and a splendid ornate mirror reflects the light from outside. There is an air of civility and charm here.

Esther returns with a silver pot of coffee, and a plate of expensive looking biscuits. When all is offered and taken, she speaks.

"This is dreadfully upsetting, isn't it? That poor woman. How can we help her?" And this natural motherly concern enables John to confide in her and so Esther learns that Alice is at least for the time being in safe hands. If she wonders for a moment how it is that John Stewart is providing sanctuary for this troubled woman, she doesn't ask why. Enough that he is concerned and is doing the right thing. Esther herself had been about to offer hospitality to Alice but now she keeps that quiet. Perhaps that might be necessary later.

"You said Esther, that you had made enquiries about Alice at Cornton Vale prison. I know she was there for fifteen years."

"Yes my dear. I have some contacts through my late husband. Medical people mainly but one of them knew the governor in the 1980's. I'm afraid it's true, the news of her conviction for murder, but it's not the whole truth. I shall tell you and the Minister what I know. Alice's conviction would perhaps not have happened today. Let us hope so anyway. Her confession of having killed her child was taken literally. The testimony of her neighbour seemed to corroborate the belief that she had killed him so that she might go away with her lover. She had heard him say that he wouldn't take Robbie. Her refusal to plead and total silence at the trial made it easy to think all this was true. The autopsy report revealed that Robbie had suffered a blow to the head and then drowned. I'm afraid that no one thought there might be another explanation, and Alice herself offered none.

After she had served eight years or so, Alice began to tell another story, to a prison visitor, a Quaker woman, and also to her father. He it was who took up her case again, and eventually, her explanation that it had all been a tragic accident was listened to, but it took a long time for any changes to be made. Her rehabilitation and contributions to helping other women in the prison led to a fresh appraisal and in 1995 she was finally given parole. She had served 15 years for a crime that never happened."

Esther's kindly face betrays the deep sadness she had felt when discovering the truth but John's expression lights up with delight. He jumps to his feet coffee spilling into his saucer.

"I knew it." His relief is enormous, "I knew she could not be a murderer. She is too wise, too lovely, she is so much loved Robbie! I knew it deep down inside myself! We must tell everybody!"

So, thinks Esther, there is something between them for John's feelings are too evident, but any further thoughts about the impropriety of this are squashed. She knows of his wife and children, and knows also that they are not currently with him and wonders why.

"Just wait a moment, John. I will ask you to keep

this in confidence please until I've asked the Minister to think what might be the best way forward. All this would be better coming from him, and not from you, for your family's sake."

John agrees, shakes her hand with renewed vigour and climbs into his jeep. He is elated at this news and decides to go back home first to tell Alice what he now knows.

The rain is set in. It streams down from the heavy sky without any change in rhythm and the ground sponges it up. The village seems deserted, only a single light in the shop as he passes by indicates life. The sound of rain whooshing and the loch waters swelling drown out all other noise.

John gets out of his jeep and unlocks his front door. Standing in the hall he senses a deep quiet.

"Alice it's me. I've come back from seeing Esther Patterson."

There is no reply. He hurriedly searches through the bungalow. She has gone. The bed is made up and breakfast dishes have been washed and dried and put away. On the table there is a note, the paper torn from the back of a wild life magazine.

John. You have been very kind but I can't impose on you any further. I've decided to go back to the croft house, you are welcome to visit me if you wish. Regards Alice.

She must have walked, John realizes, in all this rain and so he returns to his vehicle and drives to her home. He parks and knocks on the door but she doesn't answer. Worried he walks around to the back of the cottage. The lilac shutters of the workroom are closed. He stares though the rain at the nearby hillside, and then hurries to the front of the cottage and scans the loch, dread in his heart. Suddenly there is a click and Alice is standing in the doorway in a dressing gown.

"I heard the jeep. I'd got soaked to the skin so I've just had a hot bath. Do come in, John." They sit in her kitchen.

"Alice, you really ought to think about this. There is hysteria in the village and you might be targeted. It's not safe yet for you here on your own." And John wonders whether if it will ever be safe and can't stop his growing sense that beneath her robe she is naked. Her fragile appearance is an illusion however for her voice is strong and confident.

"I'm free now John and can live where I choose. I don't care what others may think of me, well most others. A few like yourself, your opinion does matter. I knew this day would come when my past would eventually be revealed. I can't escape it. I must face what comes. You've been so very kind and your friendship means a great deal to me, but you have your own reputation to think of and (there is a slight hesitation) your family."

Alice looks into John's eyes and sees the flicker of discomfort when she mentions his family. Her wet hair gleams like the petals of red tulips; the skin on her throat is creamy and smooth but he can see creases around her mouth and shadows under her eyes. He wants to take her in his arms.

"I also need to talk to you about myself Alice. I want to tell you about why I'm here, my hopes and what is happening, tell you about my girls."

"Yes, I'd like to know about your children. Later

perhaps when this is sorted but not now, not yet." She stands up and he realizes that he must leave. Reluctantly he moves towards the door.

"Is there anything you need at the moment?" he asks.

"Yes, John there is one thing you could do for me. I'd be grateful if you could bring my van back for me sometime." She finds the keys and gives them to him and smiling they part company.

***

In the village shop a huddle of women are in conference.

"I think we should find her and confront her" angrily exclaims Margaret McKenzie whose role as exposer of evil is giving her some welcome authority.

"She's up to no good coming here to hide. How do we know what she might be plotting?" Janet McCorran, behind the counter advises caution.

"She might be dangerous. Perhaps the Minister should go with some of the men?"

There is general approval of this idea though Margaret still wants to be involved. Somewhere from within, a lifetime of bitterness and frustration is welling up and in this interloper to the village the perfect target for it is to be found.

"We must protect the bairns," says another. "My Peter was scared this morning, He'd heard the older ones saying she was a witch who killed and cooked little boys."And so the mood continues.

In the schoolyard the boys of the village are also animated by the news for by now there isn't a soul around who hasn't heard about Alice Brooks. Even sensible parents who were careful not to speak about her in front of their children could not prevent them from knowing from the playground. Alistair Munro has lost his sullen stance and is invigorated.

"I say we should go and spy on her." He is thrilled with the rush of adrenalin his own thoughts produce. "We could wait until it goes dark and creep up on the place." There is a shudder of mixed fear and excitement. Small Alex Sturgeon begins to cry.

"I don't want to go. She will do horrible things to us." David Munro comforts him.

"You'll be with us Alex we'll protect you." And there grows a sense of bonding and loyalty among the boys, now eager to show themselves as young warriors avenging wrong and strengthening their newly forming manhood.

A plan is hatched. They will wait until the woman leaves in her van and then they'll go and search the place for clues to her wickedness, and that way too, more of the boys will join in.

It is decided that girls will not be allowed. Again a sense of male honour arises and they are filled with a kind of pride. The following day, a Saturday, Alice realizes that she is short of provisions and is unwilling to send word to the village store. In fact Jennie McLeod hasn't delivered post for a few days and sadly Alice thinks that she, too, might have turned against her. She will drive over to Kilsnaig for fresh food.

Alistair has been looking out for just such an event from the edge of the village, watching through the binoculars that his Uncle John had given him for Christmas and tracks the van's movements away from the cottage and heading south. He rushes around the houses calling on the boys and saying to meet by 11 o'clock at the crossroads and not to speak of the plan to anyone. He is full of energy and fervour, seeing himself as their courageous leader. David, his brother, has some doubts.

"What will we do when we get there? The place will be locked. We won't find anything. And suppose she comes back whilst we're there?"

"Oh poo you're just scared! What if she does come back? She can't kill us all!"

Nevertheless, there is a ripple of fear that even he cannot suppress and he decides to post Alex Sturgeon at the crossroads to look out for her returning van and to go for help if it comes.

The boys meet as planned, a group of nine, with Alex now in possession of the binoculars hidden behind a tree at the crossroads. The weather is dreich with poor visibility but this seems to add to the atmosphere of intrigue.

The croft house stands quietly as mist gathers around the Ben, and the loch water rocks slightly. The shutters of the workroom are closed.

"I bet that's her torture chamber!" one of the boys says and the mix of adrenalin and anxiety deepens. Alistair is trying to push the doors open or find an open window without success. He is dismayed that his plan may be thwarted. Around the back however the bathroom window is slightly open. David being smaller is called upon to climb in. He is reluctant but Alistair dares him saying that this is all about his courage if he has any.

From inside, David opens up a larger bedroom window and one by one the boys clamber in. They stand hesitating by the narrow bed. Alistair shushes them and for a minute they listen carefully; only the sound of the waters of the loch and a clock ticking somewhere. Around them in Alice's private sanctuary are photos of a small boy and on the dresser a blue cap with a green tassel.

Alistair grabs it and chucks it to one of the other boys.

"See her latest trophy," he shouts, "she keeps something of her victims!" Colin Stephenson tries it on and the tension breaks. The boys whoop and rush around the croft knocking over chairs and yelling in delight at their bravado, creating such a rumpus that it is a while before the sound of a vehicle outside stops them in their jubilation and with horror comes the knowledge that the witch has returned.

Now there is a frenzy to climb back out of the bedroom window to escape, all promises of protecting each other thrown to the wind and boys falling over themselves to get out of the house.

Alice is getting out of her van when she senses that something is wrong. Quickly she unlocks the front door and immediately sees the disturbed furniture and a wall hanging pulled onto the floor. She hears the sounds of banging and boys' voices and moves hurriedly towards its source. Half of the boys are still desperately trying to escape more than one is crying. Colin Stephenson has wet himself.

She sees that the blue cap has gone and races back to the front door and out into the now briskly falling rain. Several boys have scattered and are running away regardless of their friends still trapped. One of them is wearing Robbie's cap and Alice rages towards him, all reason gone, and flings herself at his legs. David Munro, last to try on the witch's trophy, has forgotten the cap on his head and only knows that the wild woman chasing him means him harm. In his panic he trips over one of the jetty's posts and falls into the black bitterly cold water. The chill shocks him and he plunges and gasps, his arms frantically waving. Without hesitation Alice dives into the water to bring him out.

It is just at that moment that the large 4x4 belonging to Malcolm Mckenzie races down the track with himself and both sons inside. What they see is the convicted child killer and a child thrashing about in the water with her.

With a roar Malcolm leaps onto the woman's floundering body grabbing her hair in one hand and pulling her arm with the other, twisting it cruelly, whilst his sons drag the terrified young David out of the loch. Malcolm bellows.

"You evil bitch. We'll do for you. Think you can come here and murder our bairns? You deserve to hang." But Alice has only one thing on her mind. She propels herself forward to catch a sodden clump of cloth bobbing in the water and clutches it tightly.

Other vehicles are following the McKenzies down the track. Alex Sturgeon has remained at the crossroads and stopped any village cars and sent their drivers to help. The boys are rounded up. The last driver to arrive at the croft house is Reverend McMillan who is appalled at the treatment Malcolm McKenzie is giving to Alice. He is towering over her, like a mad brute his eyes bulging with rage, prodding her soft flesh with his hard fingers, shaking her with the other hand, his face only an inch away from hers, his teeth bared. He lifts his arm to strike her but is arrested by the Reverend's command.

"Stop this NOW!" His natural authority takes over. He orders that Alice is to be put in the car where his wife will be with her and that they all must drive back to the Manse. One of the men is dispatched to fetch the police. The boys in the village are taken to their homes and parents informed about the goings-on. Alistair stands in front of his mother as she tries to comfort his brother who is shaking and crying at the same time. His wet clothes are removed and a hot bath is run. Alistair defiantly exclaims that the murderer was caught red-handed trying to drown David. Mary Munro is terrified and when David is safely out of the bath telephones her brother at the Centre. John has been receiving an order of display stands and when the call comes in he feels an overwhelming sense of dread. Quickly he drives into the village to his sister's home. The family are in the kitchen before the fire with hot drinks in their hands. David is crying quietly and Alistair has assumed his old sullen visage.

"She tried to kill our David!" he says and John has to stop himself from shaking him, instinctively knowing this is not true.

"What happened David?" he asks gently as he is moved by the boy's evident distress and bit by bit the story comes out about the boys' break-in, Alice's discovery of it, David tripping at the water's edge and Alice plunging in after him.

"Did you steal anything David?"

"No Uncle John. Well, I still had the cap on-the

one she kept from her last victim" and John knows now the truth of it all.

Back at the Manse Rachael McMillan is with Alice in a vicarage bedroom where she is being helped to get warm again. Dry clothes are produced. Rachael is doing her Christian duty but can't help experiencing a sense of aversion in helping this woman who has been in prison for killing her child. She says little and Alice even less. A numbness has come over her, not just the effects of the freezing waters but a feeling of desolation. She so nearly lost Robbie's cap, her only precious reminder of him. Her parents had organized the funeral of the boy and it was only fifteen years later after her parole that she stood by his tiny grave in the churchyard, holding her father's hand, with tears running down her cheeks. It was her father who had kept the cap safe when Robbie's other clothes, his books and toys were eventually removed from her mother's cupboard after she had died. Now Alice would not let go of that cap.

Rachael broke in, keeping her voice neutral, as she is a little fearful to be alone upstairs with this woman, for who knows what sudden or violent move she might make?

"My husband has sent for a police officer, Alice. You will be questioned when he arrives."

Rachael instinctively moves closer to the door, but Alice hardly notices. She has withdrawn into herself, into a private and safe inner place where the world cannot intrude.

Downstairs there is noise and anger. Malcolm and his two sons are still being vituperative and volatile. Revd. Roger McMillan takes control however and insists they sit down and wait patiently for the police to come. They drink some coffee in the meantime. Eventually two police constables arrive and close behind them comes a grim faced John Stuart in his jeep, and running up the drive Margaret McKenzie.

Before Alice is questioned the McKenzie men give their version of events, each eager to claim their righteous and life saving part of the drama, describing how Alice Brooks had gone berserk and was holding David Munro under water in order to drown him, and then informing the police of her criminal background. John, allowed in as he said he knew the truth of what had happened in the past, exclaims that what the McKenzies have said were all lies. Alice was trying to save David's life, not kill him. Margaret McKenzie's shrill voice rises above them all, denouncing the woman as an evil bitch.

Upstairs the two women hear the noise below. Whilst Rachael is alarmed by this, Alice is calm. John's account and the fact that his young nephew has confessed the truth is heard by the police officers and taken down in their notebooks.

The McKenzies leave, muttering sullenly. This new man, John Stewart, what does he know? Could he have threatened wee David, his nephew, to change his story? Why is Stewart so concerned about that woman at the croft house anyway?

***

At last Alice is brought downstairs for questioning. She is reluctant to speak in her own defence, merely stating that she was chasing the boys from her house after she saw what damage they had caused and that one of them was wearing her late son's cap. When that boy fell into the loch she knew he must be got out before the cold affected him. At this point the second officer is detailed to examine the damage at the croft house.

"Why should we believe you, Miss Brooks?" the remaining officer asks, "If you served time for killing your son why should you be so interested in his old cap?"

John intervenes, briefly outlining the reasons for Alice's parole and her innocence of the boy's murder and suggests that Esther Patterson is telephoned to corroborate this information.

This is done and then the first officer goes off to question David and Alistair and the other boys about the break-in. All of them are severely warned about this, but much to the parent's relief no further action will be taken. The boys are sorry yet still very frightened but at least nobody has been hurt. Privately the police officers' sympathies lie with the village folk. What right has this woman to come and live amongst them, causing trouble?

Esther, John, Alice and the Minister and his wife remain. Alice is pale and withdrawn, John is both anxious and angry. Esther now makes her offer.

"I would like it if you would come to stay with me for a while, my dear, whilst things settle down in the village you know." And where I can keep an eye on you, she thinks, for her nursing background has recognized the signs of shock in Alice Brooks.

John is relieved. He cannot possibly make the same offer, though he dearly wishes to, and the Macmillan's concur with the suggestion. John offers to return to the Croft House and collect a few things

131

Alice may need and for propriety's sake and also with some curiosity Rachael Macmillan says she will accompany him. So it is decided and Alice finds herself quietly installed in Esther's lovely home where she is given some nourishing food and then gently ushered into a pretty guest bedroom and left in peace to rest.

At the Croft House John and Rachael sit in his jeep surveying the scene. The light is beginning to fade but the mist has cleared. A cold breeze chops up the surface of the loch.

"What do you make of it all, Mr. Stewart?" Rachael Macmillan is curious. The new Director seems to know quite a lot about this strange incomer.

"Do you know her?" she asks.

John is wary, unsure how much to say.

"She is working on a commission for the new Centre," he says at last. "Mrs. Patterson is funding it, so naturally the three of us have been consulting for some while." He keeps his voice neutral. There is a pause. Rachael speaks again

"How did you discover the story of her parole?"

"Esther Patterson has contacts who knew the governor of Cornton Vale, where she was imprisoned and told me in confidence. I thought it necessary to break that trust when my nephew David told me what really happened, so that another miscarriage of justice didn't take place."

He is careful to protect his own private knowledge of Alice's affairs and there grows the realization that his situation as the new Director at the Centre might be compromised in this small community. The village folk know him to be married with a family and are expecting them to move there soon. His friendship which is how he prefers to describe it to himself with Alice, will not be understood. He is not sure he understands it either.

They enter the cottage through the front door, which is still open, and whilst John assesses the damage Rachael finds the bedroom in order to collect some clothing and toiletries. Downstairs furniture has been shifted or knocked over, a wall hanging has been pulled off its pole but otherwise little harm has been done. Thankfully the workroom had not been disturbed. In the bedroom Rachael stares at a large framed photograph of Alice and Robbie, the boy is wearing the blue cap with its green tassel and both are standing together in such harmony that tears well up in her eyes. So, there is truth in the story perhaps.

***

At Am Tealish House, Alice is lying in bed her eyes wide open but her thin body is warm and relaxed beneath the deep feather duvet. She gazes through the window at white cumulus clouds drifting by. She has Robbie's cap, dried and brushed with care by Esther, next to her on the pillow. It is now two days since the events at the Croft House and she has received much kindness from Esther in particular but also via messages of concern from Jennie, John and the Macmillans. She has some allies at least.

In the village rumours abound. At the Lobster Pot anger continues to seethe. Malcolm brims over with fury still, feeling that he has been made the villain of the piece. Customers keep their distance as he bangs and snarls behind the bar. His wife treads on eggshells. There are those who don't believe, or don't want to believe, that the woman at Lockhead croft was a victim of injustice, or that the village boys had broken the law.

Mary Monro is relieved that her sons will not have action taken against them by the local police. She has been advised to tighten her grip on their behaviour, a warning that has roused her out of her lethargy. She knows that Alistair especially could become a problem and is determined to prevent that happening. So one morning she sits them down with herself at the table and takes the matter in hand, opening up herself about the loss of her man and recognizing their grief this past year.

"Your father was always proud of you both," she says, "and had self respect too. He was a good man, an honest man, well thought of hereabouts and would want the same for you. There are those who he had poor regard for, men who had no honour, or were lazy. He brought you up to be like himself, and you are. You are good, decent boys. We must help each other. In another age you would have been at work and earning your living and helping to support your parents and siblings. Your work now is to do as well as you can at school and develop your reputation for honesty and decency. And David, you could have died in that loch. You must learn to think for yourself."

The boys hang their heads. It's a beginning but Mary knows it will take time.

"So, well, that's over now. She smiles, "shall we catch the bus into Fort William at the weekend and buy a new television?" She will put on her decent coat, Margaret thinks, and her best boots.

John is in the office at the Centre when Jim McDonald telephones.

"Good morning, John. Would you be in the office later this morning? I've received several applications for staff vacancies. Perhaps we could go through them and make up a shortlist?"

After Jim's arrival they examine applications for a cleaner, caterer and projects manager. A local woman has applied for the post of cleaner and two ladies from a nearby village for the job of caterer. John and Jim agree that if both are satisfactory a job share might be a good idea to allow for times when they were really busy and also as cover for holidays. There are three applications for project manager. John's own role as Director will also include education liaison, site management and overall running of the Centre. The project manager would have some creative input, some technological skills for display and design and help with conferences. The men go through the applications and Jim is interested by one in particular, whereas John only half looks at the forms his mind is elsewhere, thinking of Alice staying with Esther and wondering what legitimate excuse he can find for visiting her there.

***

At Am Tealish House Alice is reading in the sitting room. The well stocked bookshelves offer a varied selection of art books and catalogues of contemporary exhibitions of fine art and sculpture held in Scotland.

Esther comes in with a tray of coffee and flapjacks still warm from the oven. She is quietly and persistently putting tempting food in front of Alice, recognizing that she is a little too slim for comfort. The warmth, rest and unobtrusive care are having a healing effect on her houseguest.

"You have an amazing interest in today's art world, Esther, I'm fascinated by these photos of metal sculptures so unlike my own work, for they are hard and strong and my work is soft and pliable."

Esther replies, "I'm looking forward to seeing some examples of your work, my dear. Perhaps you will be kind enough to show me your portfolios one day? How did you come to choose weaving as your medium?"And so the story is told.

"I reached a stage in my prison term, Esther, when I was ready to be helped. My father was always there for me, and I had agreed, I don't know why, to some visits from a prison visitor called Annie. At first she just came and sat with me and spoke little, occasionally mentioning things which were happening outside the prison. She was a middle-aged woman dressed in a way you wouldn't remember later. She was plain looking, wore no make up and had an unassuming manner. Her voice was low but I noticed that her eyes were observant and her presence was calming. My reasons for being in Cornton Vale were not mentioned. The conversation was simply about how things actually were. Was I reading much? Would I like any reading material brought in? What were my interests; did I have any friends in the prison? And so on. She came once a week and I found myself looking forward to her visits. Gradually she discovered my interest in fabric design and came with articles or books that might stimulate me. She persuaded the prison governor to allow me drawing materials and paints and inks but only brushes, no pens. I played with designs and themes for fabrics and papers, and one day after reading an article about peg looms, I asked my father if he would purchase one for me plus wools of different colours. The improvement in my mental and emotional state was approved of, I was co-operative and responsive, so the governor allowed all this and from making small rugs, which I gave to my warders, I moved on to a small paddle loom and began to make patterned cushion covers and small wall hangings. Annie was always supplying me with any articles or journals she could find. I discovered she was a Quaker and I wanted to know what that meant. I'd heard of Elisabeth Fry, of course, from school days, but that Quakers were alive and well and still functioning in the modern world was a surprise. Annie was lovely, motherly, but her own person. She told me about her life and her family. Of course she must have known my prison story but she never raised it herself and in time I found myself talking about Robbie and began to cry again. I described the cap I had made for him and how he rarely took it off and Annie herself was visibly moved.

About the man I could not speak easily. I choked when I remembered him. His face came back to haunt me, the face that once I'd loved with its expression of affection and mischief. One day Annie said she could see how much I had loved him, how much I still did, and the truth of this was very hard to take. The details of those last few days before Robbie died came trickling out, slowly, with much pain, but the events as they happened were finally related. From that point

I could speak also to my father about it and he wept out of relief and also sorrow for my plight, and grief too that my mother would never know the truth of it.

Annie, who lived in Stirling, found a weaver of tapestries who exhibited work in Edinburgh but lived in Moffat in the Borders. She persuaded the governor to allow that weaver to come and talk to me about his work, and I learned from him various techniques, all theoretical of course. My skills grew, however, in table loom work and I was asked if I would be prepared to lead a group of prison women in card weaving or something similar. And so after many years I was gradually assimilated into the life of the prison. Esther, the facts about women in prison are shocking. Up to 80% have diagnosed mental health problems and neurotic disorders, anxiety and insomnia, whereas outside prison the figure is just 20%. Over half of women in prison say they have experienced abuse of some kind and younger offenders in particular, self injure in large numbers. Some prisoners serve their sentences far away from home and usually their offences are less serious than those of men, and drug dependency is rife.

Annie knew this. I learned later that prison reform had always been a central concern of the Quakers. What was wonderful about Annie was that she wasn't judgmental. She never expressed any view about my behaviour and its terrible consequences. And later still I learned this from her example. Whilst other prisoners might slag each other off and form groups who'd gang up on some poor young woman newly arrived, I could never do that. In a strange way I was given respect, which was rare. I'd served much longer than most; my crime was the worst, and I had survived. So weirdly I was looked up to and sometimes called upon to arbitrate between angry and abusive women.

Work is so vital for well being, Esther, especially in prison. Most criminals have few skills and quite a few are illiterate. They have no means to support themselves when they leave. I suggested to the Governor that a workshop be formed and sewing skills be taught and that the new computers coming in could be a way of teaching literacy and perhaps typing. Slowly some ideas were adopted but money in prisons is always a huge problem. Nearly all female prisoners and young offenders in Scotland are housed at Cornton Vale. It is overcrowded now and there is a high rate of suicide. It is terrible when this happens, everyone is affected by it. My father and Annie worked together to bring about my parole, but it took several years.

Finally in 1996, I was released and went to live with my father. I was 35 years old. After Mum died, Dad had sold the house and downsized to a flat but there was a spare room. Annie continued to keep in touch and took me one day to Moffat to visit Alan Fairbrother, a master weaver, you may have heard of him? I was taken on as an apprentice. Dad paid for it all though he had reduced his workload by now and was using the equity in his house sale. I stayed in Moffat during the week and I returned to Edinburgh at weekends.

I loved the work. Alan was very strict and often made me undo masses of weaving because of small errors. He taught me to weave images of people and I learned to dye my own wools too from natural dyes. I was allowed to undertake small commissions under supervision and later to assist Alan himself. I began to build up my own clientele and develop a style. I suppose you could say I was happy, or as happy as I could be. I loved my work but was happiest alone, finding other people a strain anxious perhaps that they would discover my past.

Then in 2000 Dad would go away on some project in the Highlands for a few days at a time. Unbeknown to me he was also negotiating to buy an old croft house there. He was thinking ahead and must have had a suspicion that in his sixties he wasn't really too well and that one day I would be on my own. Then two years later at 67 he had a serious stroke. When he came home from hospital I left my work in Moffat to look after him. Nursing help was available but a few months later he died."

Esther reaches out for Alice's hand as she begins to cry.

"Enough for now" she says.   The two women decide to go for a walk in the hills as the sun is bright and inviting. They climb slowly as Esther is not as nimble now as she once was. It is the first time Alice has seen the village from an aerial view and its layout is spread in front of her, the main street with shop, pub, manse and church, the garage and school behind with children in the playground running and shrieking, the housing estate and school house nearby. Further east just beyond the edge of the village she sees the new Centre for Highland Wildlife and John Stuart's bungalow.

After a few more days resting at Am Tealish Alice

returns to her own home and picks up her work again. She is making plans to fly to New Mexico and thence to Taos for discussions about her commission there, and she still must give thought to the project for the Highland Centre.

Jennie brings her post and supplies from the village shop. She has heard news about Alice's past and as a mother, who had also been blamed in some measure for the death of an only child, feels sympathy for Alice. Over tea and biscuits Jennie tells of her sorrows too and also of the deadness in her marriage with her man living with her as if she was merely the housekeeper. But what choice has she got? She's never lived anywhere else. The village is her life. She has no training, or skills to get work elsewhere. Her remaining years seem bleak and it's hard to deny herself the comfort of a few drinks when her man is away himself at the pub.

***

It is the Spring Equinox and the changing light also brings better weather. John is now busy planning the opening of the Centre in May and there are still interviews to be held, probably after Easter. When Alice telephones him about an idea she has for the tapestry he eagerly arranges to visit her. Things in the village are quiet now and he is, of course, seeing her on business.

She has made lunch but invites him first to her workshop.

"I've had an idea around the theme of weather, John. A design using giant rain drops falling against a background of the Ben. Each raindrop will contain an image to reflect the local community, so, one of the church, one of the school, fishing boats, sheep, the shop and the loch, a sort of composite but random picture of village life. The idea came to me when I was out with Esther on the hill. I'd use lots of grey, blue and lavender, some green and lovely umber, ochres , and sienna, so it should look colourful but not garish. I've sketched a few images here. What do you think?"

John is excited, it's a novel idea and he can see it being a focal point as people enter the Centre.

Lunch is good and the two friends are relaxed. John helps Alice with the washing up and as he stands close to her at the sink, he can feel the warmth of her body and its scent and detects an air of her vulnerability so cannot stop himself gently drawing her face around to his and kissing her. Alice responds and quite soon the two of them are making love on her bed as the afternoon sun blinks over the loch and the cerulean blue sky expands over the land.

The lovemaking is a little awkward but tender. Alice allows herself to surrender without abandon, enough for her to receive some pleasure but not to experience a loss of herself. For John, it is a wonderful release of the tensions of the last few months and a celebration to himself of his manhood. They lie together for a while until Alice stirs herself and gets dressed. John parts from her full of a new sense of hope and happiness.

He drives back to the village and goes to his bungalow and as he unlocks the door he can hear the telephone ringing.

***

In Edinburgh Kate is thoroughly immersed in her

142

studies.

To her delight she finds that she is quite a quick learner and is well liked. Her easy and attractive manner with people makes her naturally popular and her flair for design and technical competence all adds to her being on course to succeed.

But there is a growing cause for concern at home. Kirsty has distanced herself from her mother since Christmas and Kate puts this down to adolescent behaviour. Hormones, she thinks. Claire is quieter too but in a more complicated way. She doesn't enjoy her meals as she used to, leaves much food on the plate, says she's not hungry or had some cake at her friend's house on the way home from school. She has taken up jogging around the local park and makes adverse comments about overweight people.

Kate herself has never had a problem with weight and knows her figure is womanly but slim. She is proud of her waistline, her full breasts and firm bottom.

When the head teacher from Claire's school telephones one morning with a message to see her as soon as possible, Kate wonders what the matter might be.

"Mrs. Stewart, we're getting a bit concerned about Claire's weight. I don't know if you've noticed but she has gone rather thin."

"Oh, she's just stretching out before filling out, if you know what I mean, Mrs. Brown. It's normal, I guess."

"Well, I'm not so sure." Mrs. Brown wonders how it is that so many mothers can't see the obvious.

"She eats little in the refectory at lunchtime and

seems quite obsessive about sport and P.E. I think you should keep an eye on her."

Kate is upset. Surely this is just a fuss over nothing much. Better to be too thin than too fat she thinks. Claire hasn't even started her periods yet, but now cautioned she begins to watch her daughter carefully. At first she doesn't find much to worry her but after a while she realizes her daughter has taken to wearing quite loose baggy clothes, always with long sleeves and she locks the bathroom door. She wanders away from her meals or takes them to eat in her room or pushes the food around the plate or leaves the table quickly clearing the half-eaten meal into the bin. One night Kate realizes that Claire's bedroom light is on and goes to investigate. Claire is lying on the floor with her legs in the air doing bicycle movements.

"What on earth are you doing, Claire? It's late you should be asleep."

"Couldn't sleep, Mum. Thought some exercise would make me tired." So now there is a growing unease in Kate. She talks to Kirsty, asking her whether everything at school is alright for them both. Kirsty shrugs and says OK. The monosyllabic answer is all the response she gets.

One morning, however, Claire is in a state of agitation before school, having mislaid a book she needs. Kate is grumbling it's holding them all up so she rushes into Claire's bedroom and starts searching. Under the bed she finds three dishes of uneaten breakfast cereal and in a drawer a plate with the congealed remains of a dinner. Now alarm bells are ringing and the mother confronts the daughter.

"What's all this about, Claire? Why aren't you eating-or more to the point-why are you hiding your meals? And the answer stares her in the face. Claire is crying now and Kirsty stands in the doorway.

"She's anorexic, isn't she?" Kate is horrified. This has all happened so quickly. What can she do?

Kirsty is sent off to school and Kate telephones the GP and asks for an emergency appointment. Claire cries bitterly.

"Don't take me to the doctors. I'm all right. I'm just not so hungry these days."
But this isn't true. Claire is always hungry.

The GP is concerned. Claire's weight is much too low. She arranges for some specialist diagnosis. Another child caught up in this frightening syndrome. Later that afternoon Kate telephones her husband. The news from Kate comes as an enormous shock. John's feelings of euphoria are wiped away in a single moment to be replaced by a deep anxiety, fear almost. The thought that Claire is ill in this way a life threatening, frightening illness, which he doesn't understand and is beyond his ability to influence or control, affects him profoundly. He immediately makes swift plans to drive to Edinburgh and within the hour is on his way. The weather is changing and black rain clouds are moving westwards.

Kate is watching for him from the window. It is late, dark and raining heavily. The drive will have been a hard one. Indeed, John's driving is accompanied by a rising sense of panic. Rainwater is streaming down the windscreen making visibility more difficult. Outside, water is cascading down the rock faces close to the road an unreal scenario, like driving through a tunnel of water which amplifies the noise of the rain and the wind and the car engine. He can barely make out the road signs and it is only his previous knowledge of the route which enables him to keep going. Water is now collecting in huge puddles over the road surface and the bow waves as he splashes through them at unsafe speeds adds to the effect of a Red Sea wall of water around him. The car lights reflect the rushing mass of liquid. He drives as if Claire's life depends on him getting to her immediately.

Kate opens the door as he hastens towards her. "Ssh! They are both asleep. Come on through to the kitchen. I've got some hot soup waiting."

The kitchen door is closed behind them and the parents stand facing each other. Kate's face is drained and tired; she is not wearing her customary make-up and has brushed her hair back. He sees her as she really is.

"The GP has arranged a visit to a specialist an emergency appointment tomorrow. We have to watch her all the time so that she doesn't exercise or hide any food. Her weight loss is serious, John. She really is ill."

"How could this have happened so quickly, Kate? She seemed fine at Christmas, didn't you notice anything? Why didn't you contact me?" He is trying not to sound critical but the questions suggest that Kate has been negligent.

"No, I didn't notice," she says, "And where were you to know what was happening?" Both hold their breaths, instinctively knowing that this is not the best way forward. Kate has been feeling guilty enough that in her newly emerging excitement of her success at college she hasn't seen Claire's unhappiness. Or Kirsty's either. Just now she hasn't a clue about them at all.

And John is all too aware, following the afternoon's visit to Alice and his feelings about this, that he is also deserving of recrimination. He has hardly given his girls a thought for two or three months, relying on his wife to care for them, hardly even bothering to telephone for a chat. The situation is dreadful, he knows this.

"Look, John, it's very late. I've made up a bed for you in the sitting room. The girls know that something isn't right between us so it's no use pretending. We need to be honest now. We'll talk tomorrow and hear what the specialist says." And so each lie in their separate beds neither sleeping much at all.

The next morning it is decided that Kirsty will go with them too. Claire refuses to speak, barely acknowledging her father's presence, but Kirsty is tearful and her teenage moodiness dissolves as she clings to her Dad's arm and her pretence of being grown up disappears. The appointment is to be held in an office at the psychiatric unit of the hospital and as they drive in through the gate the parents' hearts sink. The place is surprisingly pleasant, however, and nicely decorated and with colourful pictures on the walls. They are all shown into the spacious consulting rooms and an attractive, well-groomed, dark-haired woman comes forward to greet them. She introduces herself as Maria Mantini and shakes all their hands.

"Kate, John, Kirsty and Claire, I'm glad you all

came. It's very nice to meet you as a family." Now she gives her attention to Claire.

"We have a concern about your low weight, Claire, and your unhappiness and together we are going to help sort this out." Her voice has an Italian lilt.

"Today we'll just talk for a while and I'll assess the situation and then we'll decide how best we can proceed. Is that OK?"

It is as if the stones lying in each stomach begin to shrink a little.

"Together we will sort this out." The words are so positive, so reassuring. Kate cries softly. John reaches out to touch her arm. Some questions are asked about the girls' school, their interests, their friends not just Claire but Kirsty too. John is asked about his work and Kate's course. Each of them outline their current situation but without mentioning the marital split.

"So John, you and your wife are living apart just now. Has that been difficult for you?"

He stiffens and is defensive he doesn't want to speak of his feelings and his reasons for them in front of his children but the doctor is too experienced not to see this and changes tack.

"Kate, you say you're undertaking some retraining for a possible new career. How has this been?" Kate is able to express her satisfaction and hopes for a more fulfilling career.

"Now I'm not going to say much more but I am going to make an appointment to see you all again here with me in a week's time and I will need to speak with you Kate and John for a minute before you go, so Claire and Kirsty if you wouldn't mind waiting outside I won't be long." Her courteous manner and equal treatment of them all is a pleasant surprise.

Alone with the parents Mrs. Mantini says that Claire is of immediate concern. She instructs them that she should not be left alone and must be at home with either or both parents for the next week. She must be given high calorie foods and be asked to eat something every two hours. Tears will flow, she warns, but do not worry. Be kind and patient and persistent. Explain that she is endangering her organs but that all will come right if she eats. Keep her bedroom door open at night. Stay in her room if necessary and do not allow any exercise. Let her watch lots of TV or videos.

Then the parents are advised that they will need counselling sessions together and separately and that an open, honest policy with both girls however difficult will be needed.

The family return home. Both Kate and John are stunned. Kirsty will return to school the next day but she is anxious too. Only Claire seems unaffected by events. When hot buttered toast and cheese are produced at lunchtime she can barely eat a tiny morsel.

"I hate cheese," she says.

"No you don't Claire. You always loved cheese. We used to call you Mousy Brown when you were little, you liked it so much."

"Well, I hate it now and butter. I'm not hungry."

"Eat a little to please me then." John pleads.

"Why should I?" the girl responds. John is taken aback.

"Because I'm your Dad, and I love you Claire very much. I want you to be well."

"I'm not ill" Claire insists, "Just fat!" Kate and John realize that the days ahead are going to be very difficult indeed.

Counselling sessions are arranged for them all and together they plan the weeks ahead. John is due some holiday at Easter and will explain to the Trustees that he needs an extended break as one of his children is ill. He agrees to return to the Centre at weekends when Kate is able to take over at home on her own. She will continue with her course but work at home as much as possible. It is a hard time. They cannot go far with Claire too much walking or exercise will reduce the small effect that monitoring her eating will produce. Kate and John therefore, are thrown together in a way they haven't experienced for many years and gradually each talk about their work and their future. When the first joint counselling session takes place John is astounded to hear how Kate feels that he has never believed that she was capable of anything much with her own life and how he had always put his own work before anything else.

At the second family appointment with Mrs. Mantini, Claire is weighed again. She has put on 12 ounces and is congratulated.

"It's a good beginning, Claire. You have done well. Now I am going to ask you all to answer a question in turn. Why do you think Claire has become so thin?"

There is a long pause, then Kate speaks out.

"I think it's because it's what girls do. It's a kind of awful fashion. There is such a fear these days about becoming overweight all the images of women, the models, the actresses and the celebrities they're all too slim or too perfect. To be shapely or motherly is deemed to be bad."The doctor listens but makes no comment. She looks at John and then at Kirsty.

The girl says, "You get laughed at in school if you're fat. Some girls make themselves sick after eating, yet they continue to stuff themselves with chocolate and stuff."

"Claire, what do you think?"

"I don't know! I just feel better if I go without food. It makes me feel strong and in control. Nobody loves you if you're fat! Fat is horrible and disgusting."

John hasn't spoken. He can't think straight. He has discovered that anorexia can kill that once the body fat is used up, the organs, the kidneys and liver and so on are raided and then will fail and once this begins the damage becomes irreversible.

He chokes out a response. "I don't know, Claire." He speaks directly to his daughter. "I love you whatever you look like. You're my lovely daughter and I don't know what I'd do if anything happened to you. I just want you to live and be happy." And he sobs, all restraint gone, in front of them all.

The doctor waits. She doesn't make any comment about any of their answers and responses. Then when everyone is quiet again she speaks.

"The triggers vary from child to child but the obsessive need for control is common to all. It's a cry for help. It can be about anxiety or love. In our society we make a link between love and food. We comfort ourselves with food or deny ourselves of it if we feel unloved or undeserving. You will get better

Claire but you must want to. It will be hard for a while. You will need to force yourself to eat but as you gain weight, little by little, you'll change how you feel about yourself. And you are well loved by your family. You will feel that too. I am not going to admit Claire to this unit today but will wait another two weeks. We've had an excellent start but I need Claire to put on two or three pounds in the next fortnight or I will admit her. Do you think you can all pull together on this?"

Kirsty puts her arms around her sister. "I'm going to help, Claire," she whispers, "I'm your big sis. You can rely on me."

During the weekly counselling sessions John and Kate find themselves wondering if the person they thought they had married had become a different person altogether. There is anger and revelation. Kate breaks down several times especially when talking about her 'affairs' as John insists on calling them. One day the counsellor asks them both if either is keeping a secret from the other. Kate declares she has told everything though she has kept hidden her feelings of rejection when her last man had left without a qualm. It is one thing saying what is happening but quite another to reveal all the emotions that have been produced.

John is silent. He, of course, has not yet spoken about Alice and doesn't wish to. What is it that he does feel about this enigmatic woman and her terrible past? Does he hope for a growing and lasting connection with her? Does he now want his marriage to end? What if Alice isn't interested in him to the extent of a lasting relationship? Is he happy to live without either woman? And what about his girls?

It has become quite clear that Claire's illness is largely as a result of the separation between himself and his wife, and her slow recovery might be jeopardised if they divorce, even if he has contact. And how could he hope that a serious commitment from Alice would be possible in the village after all that has happened? How would his girls relate to this woman and her sad past living on the edge of life?

The counsellor and Kate both sense the hesitation in John and abruptly he stands up and says he has had enough for that day, and leaves the room. He is confused. Kate knows nothing of the events at Lochhead croft and the furore in the village, and least of all, his involvement. He is, in fact, in the same position as she has been in deceiving him.

Walking on the hills that weekend, alone and troubled, he begins to see how he cannot take the moral high ground. He, too, is an adulterer the very word makes him shudder. His loving encounter with Alice didn't seem like the biblical sin. And then he realizes the same may be said for Kate. And Claire and Kirsty. Do they feel betrayed also, for the loss of trust in both parents is an unpleasant and damaging introduction to their early womanhood.

***

The following weekend he brings both girls back with him to the village whilst Kate stays behind to revise for her course examination. Kirsty is content to watch TV when John suggests a short walk on the hill behind the village but Claire who is growing stronger little by little says she will come. The day is fine a mild day with some warmth in the sun. Everywhere buds are unfolding from their tight dark knots and birdsong rings out across the hill slopes.

Father and daughter walk together each lost in their own thoughts. It has been a few weeks since John has seen Alice. Perhaps she has heard from Jennie that he has been in Edinburgh and that one of his children is ill. There has been no message from her at the office or from her home.

"Dad," Claire begins hesitantly.

"Yes, dear?"

"Have you and mum fallen out for ever?" The question jolts him.

'Fallen out,' what a strange expression, yet we talk of 'falling in love.' What is it we fall into? And when we fall out, how is it a fall? Do we think we can live in an elevated place on high? Do we fall into reality? But wasn't there a poet who said that being in love was the true reality and the rest was unreal? Am I falling? He thinks for a moment.

"Well, Claire, I guess it's more a question of losing sight of each other for a while, rather than a falling out. And I think your mum and me are beginning to see each other again now, and we're seeing a slightly different person from before and we need time to get to know that new person."

Claire is thoughtful. "Mrs. Mantini says I'm becoming a new person stronger and more my real self. She says that I have seen myself all wrong. So I suppose I have to see myself differently too. But that's scary, isn't it? Suppose if I change and nobody likes me any more?"

John scoops her up in bear hug still aware how thin she is. "Nobody could dislike you Claire who knows you. You are an amazing and lovely person." And the two return home hand-in-hand and eat some pizza along with Kirsty in front of the fire.

And so it is that at the next session with the counsellor John begins to talk about his friendship with Alice and Kate opens her eyes in astonishment as he relates that he has made love to her. Instead of exploding Kate feels a tremor of excitement that her man has it in him to feel this way and her interest in him as a sexual partner is piqued.

'Her man'. Yes, she wants to think this to be so, but she wants him to want her and her only. John can see the look of interest she gives him. They are on equal footing now he thinks to himself. As good or as bad as each other.

***

In the Centre, Jim McDonald comes in to see him.

"Good morning, John. How is your bairn? Getting better I hope." John had only said that Claire was ill and hasn't revealed exactly what was wrong just carefully saying that it was a digestive problem. Mr. McDonald is too courteous a man to pry, and continues his conversation.

"We really need to conduct our staff interviews as soon as possible. I've written to our candidates and explained the delay but I'm thinking maybe next Friday. Could you manage that John?" That is agreed.

Now that her exam is over, Kate suggests that the family all meet up the next weekend in the village. Kate knows she should get her result on Wednesday and feels that she has done well.

On Friday morning the first interviews for cleaning and catering staff go well. After lunch the interviews for the post as Project Manager take place. The first applicant, a man from Inverness, seems quite a reasonable prospect but some on the Board of Trustees have some concerns about his manner a little too brusque one suggests and perhaps lacking in the necessary people skills. Everyone agrees that his qualifications and experience are fine but there is something about him...

The next candidate is sent in and when Kate Stewart enters the room John and Jim are shocked.

"We were expecting to interview a Susan K. Miller, Mrs. Stewart."

"Yes, that is me. Susan is my first name but I've always been known as Kate. Miller is my maiden name and my professional name." Kate speaks confidently, jubilant inside at her own audacity.

Mr. McDonald looks at John and sees that this is all a surprise to him.

"I wish to be interviewed on my own merits, not because of any connection with the Director. I hope you don't have any objection", and to disallow that possibility, she sits down.

She has dressed carefully and is wearing a neat blue suit with a white shirt and just a tiny pair of pearl earrings. She has black heeled shoes and has made up her face judiciously so that the uninitiated in the use of cosmetics would hardly notice.

She sits calmly and faces the Board. Her husband is quite red in the face and Kate struggles to suppress a giggle.

"Well, we don't have any objections, Mrs. Miller." Mr. McDonald can rise to any occasion. He has already seen some advantage in employing the

Director's own wife if she is able and he has always admired women with a bit of spark.

The interview goes well. Kate is charming, knowledgeable and full of ideas. Her course is mentioned and her long experience working with the public in her previous employment. Her technical skills as demonstrated in the exam result are just what they are looking for.

John is dumbfounded. His own wife sits before him with the Trustees eating out of her hand almost. Her confidence and abilities are a revelation and he sees her in an entirely different way. What an attractive, intelligent woman his wife is!

There is no doubt in any one's mind that Mrs. Miller is the best candidate but before she is offered the post Mr. McDonald wants reassurance from John that he is comfortable with this for it is obvious that he had no idea about his wife's application. John is happy to agree.

Later that night, when the girls have gone to bed, Kate leads John to the bedroom and quietly closes the door.

The family move in together in May. It is decided to sell the Edinburgh home when Claire doesn't need to see Mrs. Mantini any more. For now, the weekly sessions continue but it will be slow progress.

There is a soft swelling of fecundity in the natural world; fresh lemony leaves bob and dance in the breeze; sturdy lambs flurry after each other on the lower slopes and the sky expands upwards, loosening its claustrophobic grip over the land. The villagers feel uplifted, hopeful.

At Lochhead croft all is quiet. Alice has gone to

New Mexico and the lilac shutters are fastened. The loch waters seem benign and Ben Dhu less formidable. White streams gurgle down its slopes defying logical pathways.

Before Alice left, John had visited the croft just once to let her know of the reconciliation with his wife. She had listened thoughtfully and had shown a loving concern, especially for Claire. He has also visited his sister more frequently, determined now to do what he can for her and the boys so that the cousins can join in village life together.

Kate gradually becomes absorbed in her new role and quietly makes allies with Jim McDonald and Mrs Patterson. The Centre will open in June and everyone is busy now. The necessary furnishings are brought in and exhibits arranged.

Sometime after his visit to Alice, John climbs the Ben from the rear car park and sits on a slope overlooking the loch and the croft. He knows now that his family responsibilities are more important than his personal feelings about the woman at the croft below him. He still cares for his wife and has been both humbled and gratified that he can now see her true qualities. He admits to himself that he has been a poor husband but isn't quite sure how that had happened. As for Alice he continues to feel a warm connection and his heart beats more noticeably when he thinks of her. And yet...somehow she was also a little far off, keeping some part of herself private, despite telling him her story. An instinct tells him that the relationship would not have gone much further but he is nonetheless disappointed.

***

One day in the middle of June, Alice returns from her extended trip to America and takes possession of her home, unnoticed by the villagers. The Centre opening has been a great success and visitors are coming in growing numbers and needing provisions from the village. The Lobster Pot has been doing brisk business in providing hot meals and accommodation. Malcolm and Margaret might even have to extend and the possibilities of winter holidays in the sun are raised. It is as if Alice has been completely forgotten.

The rhythm of the long bright days settles into a pattern. The weaver works in her studio from early morning until 3 o'clock, stopping only for a drink or to stretch her legs. After a late lunch, she steps out and climbs the Ben, avoiding where possible the strangers now to be seen dotted over the surrounding hills. Sometimes she sees John Stewart in the distance with a group of eager bird watchers and catches the flash of binocular lenses. Then she relaxes in her sitting room overlooking the glassy waters of the loch and daydreams or reads before preparing her supper. She retires to sleep still in the light. The blue cap with the green tassel rests on the dressing table and is the last thing she sees before closing her eyes. And so the weeks pass, untroubled and quiet.

One evening in August, the day following the anniversary of Robbie's death, Alice is in her kitchen preparing her supper. The door is open and outside the track to the village road winds its way like a wide strip of grey tweed. All is still. It is a perfect summer evening, unusually benign for the west coast of Scotland. She stands in the doorway basking in the beautiful soft light and, as she does so, a distant figure appears in her view. Someone is walking towards the croft house, a lone figure, a man she thinks by the shape and gait. Is it John? she wonders, then, as she focuses her attention, her knees buckle. Her body knows before her brain who it is steadily walking the path towards her. Viscerally she reacts. Her breathing stops. Her heart pounds painfully. The tensed nerve-endings in the solar plexus suddenly animate like a coiling snake. Her face flushes and her legs weaken and her mouth becomes dry. How is it, after all these long years and with all that time, age, and life's experiences can do to change a person, that Alice knows, without a shadow of a doubt, that the man heading towards her is Henry Wildgoose?

The man continues treading the path at a steadfast pace. The dark cord trousers and navy blue topcoat, which he wears, add some bulk to what was always a sturdy build and seem incongruous in the warmth of the sun. His head is uncovered, shaven still, and the intelligent eyes watch the figure in the doorway.

Alice is rooted to the ground. Nothing has prepared her for this. Surely this man cannot possibly, suddenly, emerge from a past long forsaken, mostly forgotten, certainly not consciously remembered? What had she thought might have become of him? If she had once wondered what had happened to him during those long bitter years of her incarceration, those thoughts had quickly been banished and buried deep, not to be disinterred. He had simply vanished. His name was never mentioned after her story had tumbled out to Annie and she had never seen anything written about him. Henry Wildgoose was surely dead, and this man coming towards her could not possibly be him!

But Alice knows it is so; knows the features of his face as well as the patterns of her own weavings; knows how his body moves, how the head is lifted slightly, how the brown eyes gaze thoughtfully; knows the texture of the cloth he likes to wear and knows too how her thumping heart is betraying her with an alien agenda.

"No!" she shouts. "Don't!" and she holds her arms out in front with the hands upright as if to physically push the air to form a barrier. "Go away", and somewhere comes a remembrance of these words from a long way back. And then her legs fold and she must clutch at the doorframe as Henry rushes towards her to hold her up. His arms encompass and support her and he leads her into the kitchen where she sinks into a chair. Now without control, her cries ring out:

"No, I can't bear it. This can't happen, you can't happen here, just like this. This is not supposed to happen." And the sobs choke the words.

Henry kneels by the chair and gently, as if reaching out to a child, puts an arm around her shoulders.

"My dear Alice, my dear, dear Alice. I am so very sorry." And she knows that he knows it all.

Henry Wildgoose stays on his knees on the hard stone flags until the sobbing subsides. He produces a cotton handkerchief and passes it to her, then slowly, stiffly stands up and looks about him. He is amazed by the vibrancy of the little room. The range is unlit but the late evening sun slants in from the open window lighting up the red, gold and silver threads of

Alice's hair. He looks around for a kettle, draws water from the tap and plugs the kettle in. He finds tea and mugs and then milk in the fridge, all the while saying nothing, afraid now that his coming upon her has been too traumatic. What had he expected? His recently found knowledge of what had taken place all those years ago and which had led to her incarceration in Cornton Vale prison and the imagined grief and suffering, was only sketchy. He'd discovered she was fast becoming an artist weaver but had he imagined that the past would stay in the past? Didn't he know yet that our past creates our present, which in turn shapes our future? That, in effect, there is no separate past, present or future, that the threads of our life experience weave the fabric that we become and that nothing can be unpicked?

The tea is made and Alice lifts her face to look at him as he takes the chair opposite.

"How did you know I was here? Why have you come?" He pauses to answer.

"I came back to Edinburgh to get in touch with some old contacts as I need help to publicise a deep concern I have for the plight of children and families in Nepal. I want to stage an exhibition in the West and bring the world's attention to the immense hardships and suffering going on there. So Alice, I asked about you for old times' sake. For a while no one seemed to know, then someone said you had killed a child, your child Robbie, and was sent to prison. Alice I couldn't believe it! I know how you love Robbie and would never, never hurt him." His use of the present tense underlies his incomprehension.

"So I went to Cornton Vale and was told that you had been discharged over ten years ago into the care of your father after it was discovered that Robbie's death was an accident. I was also given an address. I'm afraid I lied to get that information by borrowing the identity of a solicitor friend and talked about a legacy otherwise they wouldn't have told me. I found your old flat and had to return a few times as no one was in. Eventually a young couple opened the door and told me they had moved in after you a few years ago but didn't have a forwarding address. Then the girl remembered a catalogue arriving for you from Shetland. She remembered because of the odd name 'Floom the Loom, Weaving Supplies'. I tracked down the company who gave me this address."

Alice is calm now; her customary composure has returned somewhat. Her eyes are red and her face is puffy, but her body is less troubled. She owes him no explanations, no confessions, nothing. Her life is her own now. She does however have a right to know why he has sought her out, hunted her almost.

"And why have you come?" she repeats, unable to speak his name.

Henry hesitates again. What can he say? Surely he knows he has no justification for re-entering her life like this? He'd abdicated all rights when he left her so brutally all those years ago, knowing then that she loved him and was willing to do anything she could to keep him, even to the extent of abandoning her studies and leaving Robbie with her parents. He closes his eyes. Truly he had behaved badly then. Is he doing the same now?

"I don't quite know, Alice. When I heard what had

happened, that Robbie had died, that you went to prison, I just knew I had to see you again. I can't change anything but I want you to know how very sorry I am for the way I treated you. You didn't deserve any of it. I was selfish and cruel. I don't expect anything from you now, can't even ask you to forgive me, but ever since I came back to the UK and discovered what had happened to you I haven't been able to cope with it." This feels pathetic to him. Is he telling her that he seeks her out now because he can't cope with his part in her downfall? He must do the decent thing and get out of her life again and let her reclaim it unsullied by his own needs, his own sorrow.

Alas, Henry Wildgoose. It is too late. You have walked back into Alice's story and changed its narrative. Old emotions, deeply buried are rising and bubbling to what was an unruffled surface. There is bitterness, anguish, grief, loss, and somewhere in the background, an image of small pale daffodils swaying in the breeze.

Alice is drained. All she wants to do is curl up in bed with Robbie's cap on the pillow. The old heartbreaks are too close again. She closes her eyes. Will she never be free? Henry sees her exhaustion and moves towards the door.

"I shouldn't have come. Not like this at any rate, but I don't think I can return to Edinburgh just yet though. Will you let me come again tomorrow?"

She says nothing, feels nothing, and so Henry retraces his steps, slowly, heavily back down the track. He will reclaim his vehicle at the Centre car park from where he had been directed and try to find lodgings in the village. Her distraught face as she recognized him will haunt him for a long time.

It is light when Alice awakes having slept as if drugged, clutching Robbie's cap to her breast. She remembers yesterday's events. It feels cataclysmic; her world is knocked off its axis, the carefully made new life is in shreds now. Her thoughts replay the events of her life since leaving prison; the death of her beloved and faithful father, her exposure in the village, the aborted relationship with John Stewart the first man she had made love with for over a quarter of a century and the first time she had thought it possible after Henry and her time in Taos and the beginnings of new connections there. And now Henry himself walking in as if the last half of her life was for nothing. And perhaps it was. Maybe her life was meaningless anyway. The loch waters were inviting, enticing. She had swum in them once when she was new here one early morning to test her resolve to re-enact her son's death. The cold had numbed her and now she would welcome that closeness to oblivion. She thought she had gained some strength, some inner knowledge, wisdom even, that the prolonged suffering had borne a small fruit at least. She had relished her independence and her creativity. The welcome she had received in Taos was good, a warm bath of acceptance. She had felt validated.

And now, how was she to go on? Could she just send this man on his way? Did he really think his shame or guilt could recompense her, or Robbie, who had loved him too? No, he had betrayed her love, had cast it aside, trampled on it. His work and fame had been more important. She and her son had meant little to him, a diversion, an amusement, a conquest. In all this time he had never made an effort to find out about them. His indifference had been huge and clear evidence of his true feelings. She could never forgive him for that, for Robbie had loved Henry too and in the natural trusting way of a happy child had also recognized the man's ability to love. And Robbie had paid the highest price for this misplaced trust. Then there came that awful remembrance of holding her little boy's wet, lifeless body and her utter disbelief that he was dead, had really died, on his own, without her, and in anguish.

Steely now, determined, Alice makes up her mind to leave the village for a while. It is annoying as her work is going well but she must rid herself once and for all of this selfish, uncaring man.

At the Lobster Pot, Henry is eating breakfast. He is not really hungry and has chosen a simple meal. The rich food of the West contrasts with the simple limited fare of Nepal. The place is unattractive in the early morning gloom of the pub's dining space. There is the stale smell of beer and dogs. The landlord is clattering with barrels somewhere. The fire grate is dirty and the tables are sticky. The landlady is prying too much. Hurriedly he gets up and pays the bill and leaves. He can't sleep another night there. He is heavy with remorse and depression. Perhaps he should drive away now, leave it all. He cannot see any way forward. His mission in Edinburgh is still waiting, but he owes it to Alice to say goodbye properly this time and not to slink away. And his thoughts dwell on yesterday's meeting. How lovely she still looks, he thinks, the photographer in him delighting in the chiselled bone structure of her face so beautifully highlighted by the short spiky hair. And her willowy figure and bright clothes, they spoke of energy, confidence and a unique character. And then, how swiftly, savagely that had all unravelled before him the look of horror when she recognized him and the howl of anguish as she bade him go; her complete breakdown of composure, the racking cries, that terrible emptying of years of loss because he had appeared without warning. Henry thinks too of Alice's distinctive home and the wonderful talent she is demonstrating and developing. He had searched for her work on the University's computer and had been amazed.

He drives to the croft house just as Alice is turning her van around. The two vehicles are head to head. Henry climbs out of his car first and speaks.

"Are you leaving Alice? Shall I come back later? I would very much like to speak with you once more."

The 'once more' implies a final visit Alice thinks and sighing she switches off her engine. What is it that makes her lose her resolve? A few minutes earlier and she would have been gone.

From the western slopes of the Ben a group of birdwatchers can see the two vehicles below from their vantage points. John Stewart briefly focuses on the croft house and wonders who might be visiting Alice so early in the day. The loch gleams in the morning light.

This time Alice shows Henry into her sitting room. She needs to be in control now and leaving him to marvel at the tapestries, she goes into the kitchen and makes coffee. She is only doing this to show him and herself that she is now in full possession of herself again and can resume the normal courtesies. After returning with the drinks she looks at him with a long open-eyed gaze which discerns the changes in his face, and notices the lines deeply etched around the eyes and mouth. It is a mature face; there has been sadness she thinks but the serious expression isn't hard and sour. There is a look of forbearance, and now she sees that his right arm hangs weakly, that he picks up his coffee with his left hand.

"I think the most loving thing I can do for you, Alice, is to go away as you asked but I'd like to tell you about my life and why I have come back to the UK. Would you let me do this before I leave?"

Her silence gives permission. They each sip their coffee. "I worked for National Geographic for several years, travelling all over the southern hemisphere nations. My work was well received. I published in the States and lived in Oregon for some years winning many awards. Pictures of Crater Lake and the Pacific seaboard were some of my best work. Then in 1991, I undertook an assignment in Nepal and fell in love."

Alice's body freezes. She doesn't want to hear about this but she will not give way to him these unwanted feelings, feelings of envy and misery, but Henry understands all this, has seen the stiffening of the small muscles around the mouth and noticed the unblinking eyes and is unaccountably uplifted by this.

"I truly fell in love with the place, Alice. It is overwhelmingly beautiful and at first I could only see the magnificence of the mountains, the way they changed according to the light, the time of day, or the weather. I took hundreds of photographs. To begin with I stayed in Kathmandu and travelled from there. The city was vibrant with colour and noise and I loved the wonderful, gentle faces of the Nepalese people, so unlike the hard boisterousness of other Asian folk. I explored the villages and became appalled by the poverty I saw, and yet the people, the children especially, were so lovely, kind and laughing.

There was a 'Save the Children' office in Kathmandu and I made enquiries about their work for I had not seen that level of deprivation before. I volunteered some time to build latrines, thought I could spare a week or two maybe. I've been there for nearly fifteen years! I still took photographs though but in 2000 I lost my footing on a remote mountain slope and fell, badly wrenching my right shoulder joint out of place and breaking some bones in my wrist. The delay in getting treatment and the lack of medical expertise has resulted in the weakness in my right arm, my best arm. I can't hold much in the hand for long and I couldn't keep my camera steady and so my professional life as a photographer gradually came to an end. I shouldn't really be driving an un-adapted car here but I had to come to see you. An old colleague has lent me his.

So I became more of an administrator for 'Save the Children' based back in Kathmandu but still travelling around Nepal as and when that was necessary. I lived in two rooms in a medieval timbered building near the market place and was paid just enough to meet my needs. But Alice, things are not getting any better in Nepal. There is insurgency and civil war. I came back to Britain to publicize the plight of the people there, the ordinary families caught up in the conflicts. I have some reputation still as a photographer. I need to raise awareness with our government and the public at large. I'm mounting an exhibition in Edinburgh. I'm here for a short time and then I shall go back."

Alice is processing the information on several levels. The history of his life is one thing but the changes in his character are quite another. The old arrogance and charisma is gone. Instead there is a sense of humility but also a deep determination, a conviction in a just cause.

"Did you marry, Henry?" The question blurts out before she can stop it. It's as if another woman inhabits her mind. Henry looks at her across the table. His eyes are steady.

"I support a Nepalese woman called Nanu. After Hari, her husband, my driver and friend died seven years ago, I've cared for her and her three children. I have promised to return."

The facts are simply told. The truth and honour of it all revealed. When she had loved him all those years ago, her love was testament to these qualities as if she had instinctively known that his capacity for real love was great. Is this what loving does? Does it provide an insight into the potential goodness of the beloved and reveal a truth that delights? Is love also a projection of our own innate worthiness too perhaps? Do we see a reflection of our best selves in those we love? Whatever happened, it had not been Alice's destiny to awaken or nurture this potential in Henry and the deep, deep sadness of this floods through her body. Sorrow and loss are shaping the fabric of her life once again, and yet there is a weft of her own value for the love she made had been authentic and worthy of herself. How much of this Alice and Henry understand is hard to say. For now, they sit together facing each other, worlds of difference separating them like islands.

The coffee is cold in the mugs. When Alice lifts her head and looks into Henry's face she sees compassion and knows this is real. Without thinking she reaches out her hand to hold his hands, those familiar, always warm hands which had explored her body, and so it is that Alice tries to reassure this man who had set in motion the dreadful events which had robbed her of the best part of her womanhood. Henry is moved by this gesture of friendship. What had he missed all those years ago? Her emotional dependency had scared him; he had wanted freedom and fame.

Henry stands to leave. "I'm staying in University lodgings in Edinburgh. May I write to you? Would you visit me there? Will you tell me what exactly happened Alice? I have to return to Nepal in mid-September to get back before the snows."

Alice is calm again. His coming has broken open a deep wound and revealed a well of disconcerting and uncomfortable feelings that she will need to explore and understand. She watches Henry leave and cannot answer his questions. Will she be able to read his letters, or reply to them, or visit him?

Slowly heavily, Henry walks back along the track to his car.

That night Alice dreams. She is standing in her studio in front of its large windows. The lilac shutters

171

are folded back and as she stands there looking out, the loch waters rise and break over the track. A vast and beautiful wall of turquoise water surges towards her as high as the top of the windows and she stands transfixed with wonder. There is no fear but an indescribable and overwhelming sense of utter joy, and when she wakes up she weeps for the loss of it.

In the following days Alice sits at her loom and knows his letter will come and that she will indeed go to Edinburgh to tell him her story. The pain of it all will be relived but Alice accepts this as the price for growth, in herself and maybe in him too. Perhaps there will be a new resolution but for now Nepal is waiting for him, just as New Mexico beckons her.

The long days are fruitful. The evening light softens with delicate green and peach hues. The waters of the loch glimmer with gold and jade edged waves. Alice sits in her doorway watching the sky transmute through all the shades of pink, and silently across her vision a golden eagle slowly spreads its wings and flies with graceful majesty to its night-time roost on a mountain ledge.

27557314R00096

Printed in Great Britain
by Amazon